Break the silence, tell your truth.

SOUTH WEST POETS

Edited By Donna Samworth

First published in Great Britain in 2019 by:

 Young**Writers**

Young Writers
Remus House
Coltsfoot Drive
Peterborough
PE2 9BF
Telephone: 01733 890066
Website: www.youngwriters.co.uk

FOREWORD

Since 1991 our aim here at Young Writers has been to encourage creativity in children and young adults and to inspire a love of the written word. Each competition is tailored to the relevant age group, hopefully giving each student the inspiration and incentive to create their own piece of creative writing, whether it's a poem or a short story. We truly believe that seeing their work in print gives students a sense of achievement and pride.

For our latest competition *Poetry Escape*, we challenged secondary school students to free their creativity and break through the barriers to express their true thoughts, using poetic techniques as their tools of escape. They had several options to choose from offering either a specific theme or a writing constraint. Alternatively they could forge their own path, because there's no such thing as a dead end where imagination is concerned.

The result is an inspiring anthology full of ideas, hopes, fears and imagination, proving that creativity really does offer escape, in whatever form you need it.

We encourage young writers to express themselves and address topics that matter to them, which sometimes means exploring sensitive or difficult topics. If you have been affected by any issues raised in this book, details on where to find help can be found at: **www.youngwriters.co.uk/support**.

CONTENTS

Andalusia Academy, St Matthias Park

Siham Musse (14)	1
Rahma Sa'ad (14)	2
Khadija Wehand (14)	5
Istihar Oljoog (15)	6

Barnwood Park Arts College, Barnwood

Josh Shearing (12)	7
Robyn Franklin (12)	8
Laila Chagdali (13)	10
Rebecca Pratley (12)	11

Buckler's Mead Academy, Yeovil

Patrycja Kaczanowska (15)	12
Natasha Vickers (15)	14
Holly Lewandowski (15)	15

Churston Ferrers Grammar School, Churston Ferrers

Maya Dunford (11)	16
Sarah Jane Moseley (12)	19
Loic Bajomee (14)	20
Rose Darnley (11)	22
Summer Star Turner (12)	24
Ted Smither (11)	25
Robert Hayes (11)	26
Ben Goldsmith (11)	27
Eleanor Woodgett (12)	28
Austin Heale (12)	29
Tia Costin (12)	30
Elise Finn (12)	31

Tom Fitzpatrick (11)	32
Daisy L (12)	33

Cirencester College, Cirencester

Liberty Beswick (17)	34
Megan Griffiths (17)	36

Downend School, Downend

Jake Beckett (14)	37
Max Logie (12)	38
Jacob Pollington (11)	43
Angel Hannaway (15)	44
Melody Lomas (11)	46
Kaci-Mai Chard (11)	48
Megan Cook (11)	50
Clara Thomson (12)	52
Ethan Jones (12)	54
Mia Dagger (12)	56
Teilah Lucy Brain (11)	58
Harriet Vickers-Graham (12)	60
Roberta Eve Woodward (14)	62
Daniel A Okafor (12)	64
Siobhan Simmonds (12)	65
Phoebe Baldwin (11)	66
Olivia Johnson (11)	67
Evie Williams (11)	68
Chloe Hopkins (11)	69
Jacob Lee Rothwell (12)	70
Dan Adams (13)	71
Jacob Milsom (12)	72
Lewis Jefferies (12)	73
Joseph Adams (13)	74
Lily Seren Reynolds (12)	75
Ellen Rebecca Roberts (11)	76

Samantha Webster (12) 77
Summermay Johnson (12) 78
Hannah Hill (11) 79
Lauren James-Summersfield (12) 80
Chloe Britton (14) 81
Emily Kocinski (11) 82
Krisztian Stadinger (14) 83
Joseph Smith (12) 84
Hugo Williams (11) 85
Lily Fincken (12) 86

Fairfield High School, Horfield

Cian Estabrook (16) 87
Maya Lexie Sandiford (12) 88
Weronika Kuzniewska (16) 90
Yasmin (16) 92
Lola Hambrook (16) 94
Evan Davies (15) 96
Deborah Omolegan-Obe (14) 98
Tilly Spencer (16) 99
Eve Shobbrook (12) 100
Admas Combley (13) 101

King Edward VI Community College, Totnes

Harleigh Bradwell (12) 102
Beth Wallis (14) 105
Kyle Daniel (12) 106
Harry Green (12) 108
Hannah Wintle (12) 109
Isak Williams (12) 110
Charlotte Lewis (12) 111
Alana Pope (11) 112
Kloé Potter (12) 113
George Mathys (11) 114
Sasha Barrett (12) 115
Emily May (12) 116
Eve Widger (11) 117

Nailsea School, Nailsea

Lauren Hamilton (12) 118
Lily May Bartle-Jenkins (13) 120

Parkstone Grammar School, Poole

Maria Dodd (12) 122
Olivia Girling (16) 124

Riverside Centre EOTAS, Swindon

Max Downey (15) 126
Brooke Harmsworth-Shand (15) 128
Ash Clarke (15) 129
Leah Harding (16) 130
Sammy Hawkins (14) 131
Ellie Morgan (14) 132
Faith Taylor (16) 134
Callum Smart (14) 135
Leon Watts (14) 136
Bethany Hannah Michelle 137
Bradbury-Newton (14)
Isaac Condé Dilley (15) 138

Sands School, Ashburton

Belle Taylor (12) 139
Mae Rose Webster (13) 140
Finlay Hawkins (13) 142
Vincent Byrne (12) 143
Ben Martin (12) 144
Poppy Pugh (12) 145

St Ives School, Higher Tregenna

Keala Bewick (12) 146
Logan Cording (12) 149
Taia Christie-Beckett (12) 150
Jamie-Mai Semmons-Waite (11) 152
Kate Cann (12) 154
Archie Hart (12) 156
Lukas Poprawski (12) 158
Frankie Louise Jeffs (13) 159

Emily Bailie (12)	160
Toby Bungay (12)	161
Keala Hamm (12)	162
Eloise May Hunt (12)	163
Max Thornton (12)	164
Kyla Collier (11)	165
Wesley Veal (12)	166

Steiner Academy Exeter, Exeter

George Smith-Easton (14)	167
Kaya Ballantyne (14)	168
Alleena Purchase (13)	171
Teo 'YoungBlood' Hine (11)	172
Alitza Grace Daly (12)	174
Kama Ballantyne (13)	176
Karina Gilbert (15)	177
Laisey Jackson (11)	178

The Wey Valley School, Weymouth

Bethany Hammond (14)	179
Oliwia Schodowski (14)	180
Georgia-Louise Dorothy Genge (15)	182

Trinity School, Teignmouth

Evie Lou Daniel (14)	183
Lottie Brown (14)	184
Nevroz Turkmen (14)	187
Bertie Sweet (14)	188
Toby Roberts (14)	190
Henry Gates (14)	192
Eva Hunt (13)	194
Tom Nicol (13)	195
Lily Marder (15)	196
Oliver Protheroe (13)	197
Tom Timoney-White (15)	198

THE
POEMS

Not Ordinary

I'm not ordinary
I have many forms that I can obtain
And with them, it is easy to persuade,
Even the most difficult of cases.
I am a master of deception,
A shapeshifter if you please.
For I control a thousand personas with one click.
Like a puppeteer or a dog whisperer,
I alone decide the fate of these people,
And with such responsibility, often abuse follows.

I am the master of my own fate.
If I choose to wear red,
My people will wear red.
Peer pressure gifts me with absolute control.

I am no ordinary person.
For ordinary people do not devote their lives
To hundreds of social media accounts.
They don't own more than one phone
To control those accounts.
And they don't use those accounts to create a fake following.
I am not a catfisher.
I am just lost...
Lost for eternity in the abysmal depths of the internet.

Siham Musse (14)
Andalusia Academy, St Matthias Park

I Want To Be Good

I wonder
I wonder
Why am I not good?
Why the monster within
Refuses good
Pulls me
Forces me
Breaks the chains
Fumes, boils
Burns through my veins
I wonder
I wonder
Why I snap
Bite
Shout
Fall into a rant
I wanna be good
Kind, caring
Spread love and peace
And make hatred decrease
I want to be good
I want to be kind
I want to be the kid
The kid everyone loves

I wonder
I wonder
Why am I not good?
Even though,
I want to be good
But the monster within
Fumes
Boils
Breaks the chains
It gets hotter and hotter
Hard to restrain

Every time I try to be good
It holds
Strangles
Finds a way
It drives me
Pulls me
And leads me astray
I want to believe
I want to relieve
The world of all my stress
Anger, sadness and distress
I want you to know
I want you to believe
I send this message for the whole world to receive

If I'm bad it's not my fault
If I'm grumpy, it's not my fault
If I'm rude, it's not my fault
It's not
My
Fault

And if you want to know
What really makes me put on this show
It's the monster within
It's all its fault.

Rahma Sa'ad (14)
Andalusia Academy, St Matthias Park

Hug

Security,
Love,
Acceptance.

The feeling runs loose as they wrap their arms around you,
Happiness,
A foreign feeling,
Hope,
A job you've given up a few years ago.

Sour,
Fear,
Disgust,
Tastes that landed on the body
Push, push,
Screaming.

They hang on tight before pushing
The happiness away,
Hope has once again quit.

The river has let loose,
Ruining you,
They left you,
They will come back another day,
They will take everything from you.

Khadija Wehand (14)
Andalusia Academy, St Matthias Park

Dandelion

I bloom during the summer
Only to be blown away by the wind
Or a child
Forgotten as autumn arrives,
Blown north, east, south and west,
No one conscious of my existence
The beauty of nature's dismissed
By the urban jungle.

Istihar Oljoog (15)
Andalusia Academy, St Matthias Park

Change For The World

C hanging the world one step at a time.

H ating litter and all things dropped on the ground

A nd every day we always believe

N ever can a change be impossible

G reggs can be super nice

E ven better when it comes in paper bags

F or the scent of the food attracts animals

O ver the world, there are only thousands left

R eaching for the scent which could suffocate them

T hings will change dramatically if we get our way

H aving nearly no plastic bags until they are gone

E ven though Morrisons are selling paper bags.

W hen the same thing happens to every shop

O ver the world, everyone will be helping the environment.

R eady to save animals' lives.

L evel one now begins.

D eaths will stop and population will rise.

Josh Shearing (12)
Barnwood Park Arts College, Barnwood

I Press The Trigger Down, Down, Down

My cell walls provide no jail, for the visions I keep seeing.
They close in, they trap me
And the deceased come back to haunt me.
They push me back to the past, to the things I try to forget.
My cell walls provide no jail, for the visions I keep seeing.

My hand lifts the gun and aims into the crowd.
I press the trigger down, down, down.
The screams that haunt my dreams began...

My cell walls provide no jail, for the people I have hurt.
The toddlers, the children and the people out that day,
Stand here in my presence and will forever stay.
My cell walls provide no jail, for the people I have hurt.

The gun keeps on firing,
The people falling and screaming.
Little children cry in pain, never to see another day.

They will never leave me.
These things I did.
The pain and the deaths,
The ghosts I made.
And why did I do it?

For who?
For what?
And why?

My cell walls provide no jail for my crimes.
It provides no shelter from my deeds.
There is nowhere to hide...
I press the trigger down, down, down.

Robyn Franklin (12)
Barnwood Park Arts College, Barnwood

Change

Change, what is change?
Every time I think about change
I think of fraud and politics
I am a girl,
One in a million
A girl with a small voice physically
But a huge voice mentally.
I want to speak out
I want to be an inspiration
But there are mountains in my way.
Politics, fraud and people
But my biggest enemy is me.
I am my own enemy, yet my own love.

Laila Chagdali (13)
Barnwood Park Arts College, Barnwood

Affective

Beauty turned to destruction
Innocence turned to hatred
Love turned to fear
Happiness turned to sadness.

Comments used against people
Fear of what people will comment
People taking over
Social media is getting out of hand
It already has

Sticks and stones may break my bones
But comments will never hurt me.

Rebecca Pratley (12)
Barnwood Park Arts College, Barnwood

Stuck In The Past

"But when I was your age
I had to wake up at five.
Sun, rain, snow,
I couldn't worry.
It didn't matter at all.
Pick fresh strawberries
or anything that grew.
Feed the chickens, pigs, cows.
Then get ready for school."

"But back in my day
it took an hour to walk to school.
We didn't have a car
or money for a bus
or anything at all.
I remember once,
the snow was above my knees,
I kept going.
Why can't you be like me?"

"But when I was a young girl,
there was still a fear of war.
My house was dust, our town destroyed,
not as beautiful as before.
They had to rebuild it all.
It's a terror.
It's pain.

But you didn't go through that.
Why are you scared of such mundane things anyway?"

"But when I was a little boy..."
"But back when I was little..."
"But when I..."

'But when what?

We live in a better place,
A better time, with a better life.
We don't have to worry
whether we sold enough strawberries to eat that night.

You always think of the future
but never let go of the past.
But when will you learn that I'm not you?
That I can't do things the way you do?

But when will you learn that those fears don't last?
Why do you keep reliving your past?
Why can't you just focus on today?
At least for a while anyway...

Patrycja Kaczanowska (15)

Buckler's Mead Academy, Yeovil

Breaking Point

Ugly, stupid and disgusting;
That's what you just called that girl in your class.
Yet you don't know what she might already be dealing with at home,
Or what she might have already dealt with in the past
But you still said it, careless of the consequences.
You know that you're insecure, jealous and spiteful,
You have the power to make someone repeat
That they're worthless inside their brain.
You talk about someone to make you feel better about yourself
But it's at the expense of someone else's pain.
They feel horrible and are scared to face the world.
The playground is a warzone, where they don't feel safe.
They feel like nothing and are as strong as paper.
There's not much more they can take,
They're constantly trying not to break.
They cry themselves to sleep and just wish it would stop.
Tomorrow will be a better day,
Then again probably not.
They don't want to go out and don't know what to do,
And all of this is down to you.

Natasha Vickers (15)
Buckler's Mead Academy, Yeovil

Possible

You hide,
Hide in fear that you won't succeed,
That you're not good enough.
That everything is impossible, well...
Nothing is impossible, the word itself says
"I'm possible."
You're possible,
Don't shrink yourself,
Don't hide,
You're braver than you believe,
You're stronger than you seem,
You're smarter than you think,
You can accomplish anything,
Be true to who you are,
Believe in yourself,
You are good enough,
Don't listen to the downers and the haters,
Shut out the negativity,
You are loved,
You are important,
You are capable,
You are possible!

Holly Lewandowski (15)
Buckler's Mead Academy, Yeovil

The Forgotten Children

We were taken, taken from our lives,
Treated as lesser people,
We were young and we had fun,
But then we were stolen, taken.

The silence, the now empty halls, the wooden beds,
And the bug-infested floors.
We lived at this camp, a place, not a home,
With its horrible soldiers and its inhospitable rules.
We lived in fear, terror and sadness,
Scared that every day would be our last.

Many died, some survived,
But we will always be here,
Whispering, waiting,
Waiting for the next.
And our bodies piled into pits,
Killed in the gas chambers,
Shot without mercy.
We were the brave, the scared and the sad.

We were denied our childhood,
We were denied our happiness,
And worst of all, denied our family.
And every night the survivors cry for us,
But we are left; in the ashes, the wind, the dust.

And though we may have made our sacrifice,
Listen to our call:

For we are those who survived through it all,
The pain, the suffering and finally death.
But in our no longer beating hearts, we know we shall not
rest,
Until we are known and are remembered, and remember
this.

We were normal children, born just like you,
Laughed just like you,
And played like you,
But we were different, destined not to grow up,
Not to become our dreams.

We were the doctors, the scientists, the teachers of the
future.
And yet our lives were ripped away
From beneath our own, calloused fingers,
Those so sore from labouring away at camp,
Our lives were burnt like paper to a flame,
Too quick for us to understand,
Because we were normal children like you,
But we were destined to die as children.

And so we stay, watching, whispering,
And waiting for the next,
As we were not the last.

War still happens, people are still killed for who they are,
Or what they believe in.

And yet, how can people be so cruel to others,
And kill them in cold blood.
And now as we roam the camp's empty halls,
Listening to its silent screams and moaning calls,
We remember our lives so dear,
For we were the brave, the scared and the sad.

So remember us all.

Maya Dunford (11)
Churston Ferrers Grammar School, Churston Ferrers

The Woman In The Window

The person you notice but at the same time don't,
The woman in the window,
The one in the corner, wanting to be left alone,
The woman in the window.

She leaves the café, having finished her coffee,
The woman in the window,
She sits by the bus stop, purse in hand, but never boards a
bus,
The woman in the window.

You will never know her name,
The woman in the window,
But she will seem to follow you everywhere
The woman in the window.

You will never notice her but at the same time you will,
She will seem like a ghost, there but not there,
She will stare into space, dreaming in her own world,
Where life does not treat her in the cruel way this one does,
The woman in the window.

She will be there, everywhere, every day for years and years,
Then she will disappear, she will have lifted herself
Off the bottom rung or perhaps something slightly more
sinister.
She will know you but you will never know her,
The woman who is everywhere but here.

Sarah Jane Moseley (12)
Churston Ferrers Grammar School, Churston Ferrers

Welcome

Welcome to our country.
You're welcome here.
We should never say,
"No, you can't be here.
Filthy scum taking our jobs,
We take priority."

Let's look at ourselves,
All we do is look down on these people,
As if they're ruining our population,
Bringing disease,
But maybe we're the disease.
Being patriotic, a germ in our blood,
If we were in their position,
What would we do?
We would bow down and pray to our gods,
Our lords,
As our men and women may die for us,
Against an army of evil.

Then where will we go?
All other countries are telling us no,
We try to find jobs,
To feed our families,
So we're stuck being exploited,
Prostitution, little paid labour,
People pulling our strings like we're their puppets

Punch and Judy, Basil Brush,
We'd be their workers, their playthings and their pets,
What would we do, fight back and be deported?
No,
We'd work,
We'd fight through the pain,
For friends,
For family,
For us.

So now as we say no,
Think as if we were in their shoes,
And look at their pain, their anguish,
Before you raise the plague of being patriotic.

Loic Bajomee (14)
Churston Ferrers Grammar School, Churston Ferrers

Alone

There was a time when I was alone,
No friends, no family or even a home.
No one to love and care for me,
Less food and drink than other families.

Night after night I closed my eyes,
Watching the stars shoot through the sky.

Slowly I walked to the market square,
Hoping for once that someone would care.

Then came my chance.
I opened my mouth to say the words,
That could save my life.
Too shy to say the lines.
A different voice behind me whispered,
"Are you okay?"

Those three words boosted my confidence.
"Yes," I said feeling better than I had been in years,
For someone had noticed me, someone kind,
Who saw me as an equal, instead of an alien.

He never stared at me or asked too many questions,
Like people always did.
He gave me a warm blanket and some food,
And asked me if I wanted to talk for a minute.

After ten minutes, which seemed like five seconds,
He had to leave me to go back home.
A realisation came to my mind.
If there were more people like him,
The world would be a better place to live in.

Rose Darnley (11)

Churston Ferrers Grammar School, Churston Ferrers

War Poem

We used to be chased around the house by our relatives,
But now we're here, we are your captives.
I'd packed my clothes, only my best,
You wouldn't let me take the rest.
I left my friends, everything I know,
I really wish I didn't have to go.

You don't have to pretend, I know your motives,
You treat us like we're different, 'natives',
My tears are all over my dishevelled face,
You beat us, kill us because of our race.
We work every day, on field and farm,
Just so we don't come to harm,

The smell of death, thick in the air,
You shaved us of all our hair
And took our money, gold and memories,
Some of us have been here for centuries.

"If you work hard, you will be free,
You're not our heroes, you're our abductees."
You kill us daily, one by one,
One day, it'll be my time to run,
From this place, far away,
From this place, I spent every day.

Summer Star Turner (12)

Churston Ferrers Grammar School, Churston Ferrers

The Holocaust

The Holocaust, it was a horrible time to be alive,
Over six million died,
Whoever went through this, I feel so sorry for you
For what you went through.

It must have been hell when you heard the bell
To get on the train,
It was no game.
People were shot,
And that would have hurt a lot.

They lost their family, they lost their everything
I can't believe this could have happened
To someone or something.

It was a horrible period of time
There were millions of lives on the line
And not many people survived.

Anyone who survived
I give my praise to you
Over everything you went through

It must have been horrible
I don't know how it was possible
But all I know is that you're very lucky
To be alive and to have survived.

Ted Smither (11)
Churston Ferrers Grammar School, Churston Ferrers

We Have A Voice

No one strives for equal rights
Instead, we all just get into fights
While we all take our different flights
The anger and hatred still bites

We never let past experiences go
Oh, how I wish our lives could just flow
Instead, hatred burns inside of them
They don't care how it will end

Unsafe places,
Dangerous face.
Our world lies in despair
As we treat each other with rights so unfair.

Evil people with dastardly ideas
While their victim neverendingly fears
They destroy and kill
And our cemeteries start to fill

But we have a voice and we can speak
We can stand up, it will be so peak
So who's with me, let's destroy this pain
We are not in it for glory or fame.

Robert Hayes (11)
Churston Ferrers Grammar School, Churston Ferrers

The Holocaust

My head is shaved bare
Just like Germany was shaved of the Jewish
I'm standing here in the rain
The rain from the country I used to belong in
The rain I'll never see from my home
The home that I was brushed from
Just like bugs in the Nazis' eyes
The Devil's pets.
I may not be perfect but I know for sure
I'm human
The one that used to walk alongside nature
The one that was able to walk outside without being
shouted at
But now these broken and twisted wires in front of me are
holding me back
Not letting me leave, enter into the world
And not this mound of horror
Moulding and shaping people however they want
Giving them the shower of death
The one I shall take
To leave this world of hatred.

Ben Goldsmith (11)
Churston Ferrers Grammar School, Churston Ferrers

It's Fake

Dear Sorbet,

I do admire you so much,
You are kind and I enjoy your cold touch.
You are my favourite and my best food,
You're so tasty and always lift my mood!

Oh, dear Sorbet, how I love you a lot,
Always there for me when I'm in a strop.
Although you have left, you remain in my heart,
I really feel upset when we're apart.
I would never ever want to depart,
And just know you will never leave my heart.

You will always and forever taste best,
Even pizza dinner and all the rest.
You are so super and good for summer,
You're even better than our next plumber!

Eleanor Woodgett (12)
Churston Ferrers Grammar School, Churston Ferrers

Global Warming

Trees are falling,
Plants are withering,
Temperatures are climbing,
Animals are dying.

Who is to blame for this?

We are the ones clearing the trees,
We are the ones killing the plants,
We are the ones causing temperatures to climb,
We are the ones driving animals into extinction,

We are the ones destroying the world.

How do we stop this crisis?

We stop using fossil fuels,
We stop cutting down the trees,
We try to stop using greenhouse gases,
We stop destroying animal habitats,

We restore the world to its natural glory!

Austin Heale (12)
Churston Ferrers Grammar School, Churston Ferrers

Nothing Left But Me

I felt so scared
All alone
No family
No place to call home

No hair
No friends
No childhood
This list of misery doesn't end

They took what I looked like away from me
They took who I could have been away from me
But they couldn't take love away from me
As I still love my family very dearly

No matter how many scars
How many beatings
How little food
How little water

My soul and my spirit
My heart and my mind
Myself on the inside
Still survived
Even in those terrible times.

Tia Costin (12)
Churston Ferrers Grammar School, Churston Ferrers

Our World

Our world is split in half,
From good and bad
The brave and weak
Poor and rich

But no one started out like this,
We all had the choice
It was ours to make
And yet, those who are richer are not better,
Those who are weaker are not wrong,
Those who are smarter are not braver.

Everyone is different,
You'll just have to accept,
That not everyone had the same opportunity
To be free
To be the same
To be equal.

Elise Finn (12)

Churston Ferrers Grammar School, Churston Ferrers

Scales

The scales are unjust,
The wealthy men weighing it down
They say it'll be fairer,
When I mention it they just frown.

The scales are unfair,
It won't change just by my will
It might never be fair
The scales shall stand still.

Unmoving they've stayed still
So long have we tried to thrive,
Some attention, some free will,
To help our side survive.

My will alone will be ignored.

Tom Fitzpatrick (11)
Churston Ferrers Grammar School, Churston Ferrers

Rocking On The Deep Blue

Rocking on a boat,
In the deep blue.
On my own,
Far-off from everything.
The waves,
Gorgeous.
Unique.
But of course, I'm a refugee.

Daisy L (12)
Churston Ferrers Grammar School, Churston Ferrers

Humanity

Here one minute, gone the next.
The stars check their watches,
Watch us hurtle through nothing,
Worshipping a candle.
Shakespeare and symphonies,
The Rosetta Stone and motorcars.
We are dandelions in cracked pavements, drips
From an icicle upon snow-covered grass.
We called ourselves "Sapiens".

We are problems, particles, pages of books
On the streets of a floral city.
Stories passed on in the truth of the night. Reactions.
The pressing air can feel our hearts beat,
Falter, sigh. The light that flows along our river beds
Has made its accidental home here.
Trees whisper our lives.
Time will be forgotten
Before the burning candle is snuffed.

The elder by the watermill
Has been taken by glass and metal.
Ancient beasts swirl overhead.
We are insanity as we jump, fall,
Climb.
We passionately cry, bravely fail.
Quietly, waves lap at the bright horizon.

Hours are an anomaly created by a mistake;
One day falls

Into the next.
One blink in the eyes of the universe.
We looked at the skies and imagined heavens,
Looked down at our feet of clay and saw gods
As the paradise around us wilted.
Sparks ignite us, fire ends us.
We have flames in our eyes.
The thundering grasses rise until we are nothing more than dust.
Perhaps the cave paintings will last.

Life lingers on.

Liberty Beswick (17)
Cirencester College, Cirencester

Ignorance

Everybody only ever wants you to be safe,
Ignoring everything
Everything that can be used to keep you safe.
They ignore the cries for help,
All in exchange for the perfect image,
No matter what they insist.
Pushing it away as anything else.
Like the mounting scars upon your wrist
Aren't by your hand.
But instead something mundane,
Normal, perfect - almost.

They look at your tears of woe,
As a confusion of your own feelings,
Towards someone you love,
Who they swear is only a crush,
All because, God forbid their child loves someone,
He, she or it.

They always insist to know what's best for you,
Every time.
Repeating the same words.
Leaving you to be driven to this point.

A point of solitude, completely unknown
Oblivious to the real world.

Megan Griffiths (17)
Cirencester College, Cirencester

D-Day

They all stand in solitary silence,
remembering their last memories of their loved ones.
As they all draw close to the enemy in valiance,
all wanting peace and to reunite with their daughters and
sons.

They couldn't tell where the grey skies ended,
and where the grey seas began.
Grey clouds swirled in a tumult of stormy air above.
Blue-grey waves swished below,
crashing into the side of the iron grey boats.

The beach stretched out alongside the water,
where everyone landed, shaking in terror,
both sides engaged and fought through the slaughter.
Screams filled with agony echoed through the day.

There was no compassion between them,
bullet after bullet, in all effort to kill.
Weeks of suffering and slaughtering passed.

Everywhere was red, even the ocean's tide,
the atmosphere was quiet and lost.
They all laid in silence, waiting in a better place to meet,
with their loved ones, once again.

Jake Beckett (14)
Downend School, Downend

Journey To Secondary School

In my first year of school, my life was full of fun,
I was in a class called Reception.
I would go to school with my mum
She would take me to Reception.
One day I met a girl,
She would take me to a room away from Reception.
Once we were away from the teachers,
She would teach me how to spell,
This happened every day in Reception.
In my first year of school, my life was full of fun,
I was in a class called Reception.

In my second year of school, my life was full of learning,
I was in a class called Year 1.
When I came to school, I learned that the girl
Had spent two years in reception and as I learned that
I thought all about the spelling ambitions I was deserting,
She was in Year Two and I was only in Year 1.
So, I made a new friend,
He was also in Year 1.
We vowed we would be friends until the end,
Little did I know about my misshapen future,
Since I wasn't a fortune teller and I was only in Year 1.
In my second year of school, my life was full of learning,
I was in a class called Year 1.

In my third year of school, my life was full of work,
I was in a class called Year 2.
Our teacher made us work until it hurt,
Reception and Year One were unlike Year 2.
But soon I made a second friend,
Unfortunately, I made no others in Year 2.
My friend, like me, seemed to be unaware of the class'
trend,
And I also got a pair of glasses and met an *awful* kid
Who ruined our class' 'marble parties' all in Year 2.
In my third year of school, my life was full of work,
I was in a class called Year 2.

In my fourth year of school, my life was full of playing,
I was in a class called Year 3.
I stopped playing with my first friend because of all the
anger
He and my second friend were displaying,
This choice would change my life in Year 3.
I obtained my 'Pen Licence' in this year,
I befriended the 'awful' kid and a boy, also in Year 3.
And when my second friend obtained his 'Pen Licence' too,
I was proud of my peer,
We played happily for the rest of Year 3.
In my fourth year of school, my life was full of playing,
I was in a class called Year 3.

In my fifth year of school, my life was full of suspense,
I was in a class called Year 4.
My group of friends played together, normally,
Playing heads or tail with two pence,
But I was beginning to drift away from my friends,
I began to think I would be alone
For the rest of my life at Year 4.
Then I learned that I was moving to a new house,
But I didn't want my friends to know,
So I kept it a secret throughout Year 4.
Then a few weeks before the move, I finally told my friends
And I felt as vulnerable as a mouse.
On my last day in Chippenham,
I went to my first friend's house, he was in tears,
So I felt so guilty about leaving him in Year 3,
Since he still liked me after all the things
That happened in Year 4.
In my fifth year of school, my life was full of suspense,
I was in a class called Year 4.

In my fifth year of school, my first year at my new school,
My life was full of confusion,
I was in a new class called Year 4.
On the first day of my new school, I made a friend
And learned about exclusion,
And I kept that friend for the rest of Year 4.
I only had two terms but I learnt a lot,
Such as linguistic devices, friends and foes,

The fighting and my unbelievably outstanding intelligence,
All in Year 4.
I thought I could defend myself,
But these children in my class and only my class,
Made me look like a very fragile, clay pot.
I learned that these children made the 'awful' kid
Look like an ordinary person
And the less-strict-than-my-old-school Code of Conduct
I should follow, all in Year 4.
In my fifth year of school, my first year at my new school,
My life was full of confusion,
I was in a new class called Year 4.

In my sixth year of school, the second year
At my new school, my life was full of adaptation,
I was in a class called Year 5.
My friend and I grew apart since he didn't give me
Anything back from him, not even a birthday invitation.
Then I met another boy and I was friends with him
For the rest of Year 5.
But it wasn't all 'nicey-nicey' with him, he was training me
In how to defend myself, and there were fights
Between classmates throughout Year 5.
Then I was involved in some, I lost each of them,
So my mum and I decided that I should do
A martial art called Tai-Kwan-Do so I could defend myself
From my class' might.

After that, my timeline became less bloodstained
For the rest of Year 5.
In my sixth year of school, the second year
At my new school, my life was full of adaptation,
I was in a class called Year 5.

In my seventh year of school, the third year
At my new school, my life was full of happiness,
I was in a class called Year 6.
When I broke up with my friend, I embarked on
A lonely journey that I called 'friendlessness',
I endured this journey until term two of Year 6.
Then my old friend and another boy
Asked me to play basketball,
Then I became best friends with them even after Year 6.
Then my best friends and I met two boys,
Who always bragged, "To play with us,
You don't even need a ball!"
We played lots of games together until we had to say
goodbye,
One of the boys was going to a different Secondary school
At the end of Year 6.
In my seventh year of school, the third year
At my new school, my life was full of happiness,
I was in a class called Year 6.

And at my eighth year of school, my first year at Secondary,
It's an exciting new journey!

Max Logie (12)
Downend School, Downend

My Mental Health

My mental health matters!
My mental health rules my body and self-esteem
It makes me feel ecstatic on one day
And then crushed on the next
When I lose control of my emotions
My heart starts thundering like a Formula 1 racing car
Zero to sixty in three seconds flat!
Banging like an angry revving engine
Inside me, a frightened animal awakens
Like a deer trapped in the headlights of a car
Alert, alone, alarmed
After that everything goes black...

My world is crushed
Finally, I start to calm
Those horrible thoughts begin to blur
Daylight starts to seep in, flooding my eyes
I start crying and the mist begins to lift
What will tomorrow bring
And how will I cope?

Jacob Pollington (11)
Downend School, Downend

What I'm Trying To Say

Self-serving, self-absorbed, cynical self-worth,
We hate our reflections and love money first,
"Look what I own" is all that you need,
Go ahead then, show them just what you mean.

We are vessels for love, creation and joy,
But what is your worth in a fancy new toy?
Stop your obsessions and look at your life!
Take in all the wonders of being alive.

You're as stupid as you look - as mad as a cow!
To drown in vanity, well look at you now!
Don't you think you'd go back in your life if you could?
Well, let me show you just why you should.

You think you're the lead of some Hollywood story,
Well, I've got some news, please take it slowly,
It's not that I hate you, no really, that's crazy,
But the extent of your intelligence seems a bit hazy.

Each life, each mind, each person on this earth,
Has a mind so vast it would cause you to burst,
You see my own face and it tells many lies
Do you understand the struggles in hiding outside?

The shine of an apple cannot always hide the core,
Eventually, it rots and beauty shows no more,

Let me put this in a way you'll understand,
A jewel that is shattered cannot be sold to Man.

Look, I know it's harsh but what I'm trying to say,
Is I love you, I love you, I love you all the way.
So why is it you'd rather stare at a phone,
Than grab those three little words and make them your own?

Stop.
Breathe.
Look at me now.

I'm not perfect or prosperous or properly pure,
But I'm here and I'm real and soon I won't be any more,
So take it all in as best as you can,
What I'm trying to say is, hello, here I am.

Angel Hannaway (15)
Downend School, Downend

The Christmas Truce

It was a Monday evening,
on a cold and frosty night.
The midnight moonlight glistened,
and the soldiers froze with fright.

Gunshots as loud as drums,
crackling through the air.
The soldiers were almost deafened,
yet they did not care.

Soldiers were in agony,
they cried so very loud.
Their lives would soon be over,
at least they'd made their family proud.

Then they started singing,
it filled the trenches with joy.
A Christmas song to lift their spirits,
from when Jim was a little boy.

There were two brave soldiers,
who were fed up of the war.
Just for Christmas Day,
they wanted no more.

His fingers as cold as ice,
shivering in the air.

Jim stood up with worry,
and then he did not care.

Germany and England were united,
Otto and Jim shook hands.
To make a merry Christmas,
they stepped on each other's land.

Then they played a football match,
everyone joined in.
The ball flew like a bullet,
and England scored the win.

Bombs were heard,
it was time to go.
They were like a pack of cheetahs,
sprinting in the snow.

Silent, sitting soldiers,
shivering in the cold.
In the trenches they were,
with the small ration that they hold.

Before they went back to the trenches,
Jim gave Otto his coat.
In Jim's coat pocket,
Otto found a chocolate bar.
This little act of kindness,
was the kindest by far.

Melody Lomas (11)
Downend School, Downend

Plants Vs Seasons

As winter falls across the earth,
the plants all wither and die,
from now until spring this is the birth,
of the plants who don't say goodbye.

The snowflakes land on the softening soil,
watering the roots beneath.
The vines suddenly begin to coil,
covering the empty heath.

Then the winter begins to pass,
leaving the leaves to grow back.
Pollen and leaves fall onto the grass,
deciding to abandon the pack.

The grass becomes a lively green,
and all of the plants thrive.
The bees get pollen from where they've not been,
before returning to the hive.

The summer comes to brighten the day,
leaving all coldness behind,
the heat leaves plants in heaps of dismay,
as this disaster is one of a kind.

The blistering heat leaves the grass pale,
and the leaves start to wither once more,

as the sun's heat turns to betrayal,
as the water supply is surprisingly poor.

Then autumn comes and the leaves turn red,
allowing true colours to shine,
plants coil and wither instead
of owning the colours as thine.

The frostbite comes round, intentions clear,
producing for plants agony and pain,
showing plants who have survived all year,
that they have finally been slain.

Kaci-Mai Chard (11)
Downend School, Downend

The Boy With No Name

Upon a bench,
Wooden and brown,
Alone he sits,
With a big wide frown.
As lost as a lone sheep,
You would never hear a peep,
From the boy with no name.

Cold air blew in his hair,
The wind whipped in his face,
Leave his bench,
He wouldn't dare.
As lost as a lone sheep,
You would never hear a peep,
From the boy with no name.

Kicking dirt beneath his feet,
The field was a blank and empty sheet,
Thoughts running through his mind,
Leaves fell from the tree behind.
As lost as a lone sheep,
You would never hear a peep,
From the boy with no name.

Alone in his head,
Finally, a tear was shed,
He sat for a while,

No one has ever seen him smile.
As lost as a lone sheep,
You would never hear a peep,
From the boy with no name.

One summer's day, he took his usual seat,
A little shadow was coming close,
This made his heart complete.
As lost as a lone sheep,
You would never hear a peep,
From the boy with no name.

The lost little sheep was starting to see his way,
When a young blond boy came along to play,
"What is your name?" said the blond boy after a while,
He thought about it and then replied with a smile,
"My name is Harry."

Megan Cook (11)
Downend School, Downend

The Human Race Is Not As Innocent As You Think It Is

The human race is not as innocent as you think it is.
Not everyone is aware of the effects we cause every day.
I hate the way humans destroy the world
through landfills, pollution of the sea and global warming;
this is not the way.

How cutting down trees (which destroys animals' homes)
just for paper is acceptable
and leaving bottles, tubs or lids on the floor to be washed
away at sea is okay?
You know it might, at this very second, be eaten by an
innocent animal trying to find food.
This needs to be stopped, this cannot be the way!

Violence is taking place at every moment,
from a small punch to a life-threatening fight,
this is why guns need to be banned and any sort of horrible
fighting needs to be stopped.
"It's no big deal. It happens every day. It will be alright!"

Some people aren't as fortunate as us.
Some only ask for water or for food,
then we go and ignore them.
Our behaviours are so rude.

In the end no one listens.
We need to make the change.

What is life going to be like in the future?
I'm guessing it's going to be strange!

Clara Thomson (12)

Downend School, Downend

No Place Like Home

Deep in the city
Where you and I don't go
Down an old alleyway
Lives a small man called Po.

Every Monday morning,
He trudges down the street
In his old grey muddy boots
That have never fit his feet.

To the cheap little corner shop
The man walks on and on
Passing parents with their kids
Soon those days will come...

He heaves open the metal door
That rings the little bell
He shops the store for all his goods
Then joins the long queue, "Oh hell."

As soon as you know it, he's out the door
His money falling from rips in his pockets
Wanders back down the street
Kids running past like rockets.

He turns the corner into his house
But not through a door

Through a small gap in a fence
That others would ignore.

The man lay down on a cardboard
Pulls his blanket over to sleep
Then slowly closes his eyes
And begins counting sheep.

Deep in the city
Where you and I don't go
Down an old alleyway
Lives a small man called Po.

Ethan Jones (12)
Downend School, Downend

The Movies

As I sit in the cinema,
the lights slowly fade away.
The room is silent as we wait,
wait for the screen to light up.

The opening music blares out,
out of the speakers that surround us.
The screen lights up the room,
people's eyes are glued to it,
not daring to look away.

Everyone gets lost inside the movie.
It feels like hours that we've been watching,
watching the actors act,
and convince us we're there with them.

A tingle runs down my spine,
I can hear quiet sobs in the audience.
Smiles spread across people's faces,
as their eyes follow the actors across the screen.

The engaged audience break out in laughter,
once they hear an amusing joke.
Every time a jump scare appears,
everyone is in shock but quickly laugh it off.

Darkness.

The jaw-dropping film has ended,
as the end credits flash on.
The inspired crowd of people begin to exit,
as the lights flicker on.

Mia Dagger (12)
Downend School, Downend

Dear Alice

Dot to dot, it's ultimate,
But nothing is better than you,
Not even a unicorn or two.

If you were a film,
You're better than It.
Even better than SuperMario 8-bit.

You and I love to game,
The games we play are on top of fame.

My love for you is stronger than words,
The amount of love is like an animal herd.
When I see you, what changes is my mood,
I love it when we share our food.

I just wanted to say,
You and I are like diamonds in the sky,
A vision of ecstasy I see,
Shine bright like a diamond.

I just can't stop thinking about you,
Dreaming and writing about you.

You're the missing piece to the puzzle,
To stop my head getting in a muddle.

You're the last in the jigsaw but next to me,
Others are like, "Omg, is she with he?"

I'm cooked, you're raw,
You are the one I like to draw.

Teilah Lucy Brain (11)

Downend School, Downend

Equality

Equality?
What does it mean?

It means to walk the streets happy,
With black and white,
Male and female,
Young and old,
Gay and straight,
European and American,
Muslim and Christian.

Walking together,
Free of status and restrictions,
No higher, no lower,
No one better or worse,
The only difference,
Are our beautiful and unique gifts,
And our wonders.

No traditions,
No feudal systems,
Keeping us apart,
All laughing,
All playing,
All working,
Together.

Everyone,
Dancing until the end.

No one mistreated,
Past is forgotten,
Only us,
Dancing,
Dancing through the storm,
And into the calm.

That is my passion,
For all of us,
To work together,
Until the end,
And someday,
Somehow,
We will achieve it,
No matter what.

Harriet Vickers-Graham (12)
Downend School, Downend

Vanity

You are doing it for attention
It's all in your head
I am silenced
But inside it's dread.
I am terrified
My thoughts are scenarios
I am scared of the unknown
Scared of myself sometimes
Fear eats up my insides
Strangles me from within
I don't need sympathy
I need help if I can
Brave myself up to admit it.
I am a self-destructing worrier
And I can't stop it.
I need attention, not for vanity,
But so I don't break inside.
Tears are oceans and screams are battle cries,
From the war in my head.
And it's a brutal one,
Blood is spilt and it will never be clean.
Blood will have blood,
I will pay the price.
I am dangerous but everyone thinks
That I'm just nice

Smiles can fade
A mask is worn and comfort torn
And all you saw was vanity.

Roberta Eve Woodward (14)
Downend School, Downend

Football Poem

As I walk in the crowd,
They are extremely loud,
The sun was out,
I couldn't see the clouds,
As they clap their hands,
With joy in the stands,
We were all dripping,
Out our sweat glands.
As the ref picks up his whistle,
I gave the football a tickle,
It goes to the player,
I pass the ball to Crayer,
He gives it to Soul,
Bang! He scores a beautiful goal!
One to Chelsea and zero to Liverpool,
The crowd go wild,
Soul with a big smile,
Mo Salah takes the kick off,
Just saying his boots look like a rip-off,
He passes it to Mané,
Mané crosses it down the line,
It doesn't matter because it's full-time!
Chelsea are the winners!

Daniel A Okafor (12)
Downend School, Downend

Deforestation

D ictionaries preach it's merely 'clearing'
E ven though it's so much more
F orests rapidly disappearing
O nce abundant in life but now like war
R avenous machines lurking in woodland earth
E xtinction engulfing a species-rich creation
S ociety stealing nature's turf
T ropical havens, sacrificed with no appreciation
A micable citizens strive for the proper conduct
T rying to prevent the commercial caused crime
I ndustries might oppose and therefore erupt
O r trees will perish within a time
N othing can stop deforestation, except mankind's
realisation.

Siobhan Simmonds (12)
Downend School, Downend

The Homeless

The homeless don't have their life at their best,
That's why we need to help them rest
Give them blankets, cushions and food
To help them survive the treacherous night through.

As I watch people walk past them on the street
With no thought to how their days and nights are so bleak
I am washed over with guilt at the thought of another cold night
Why do we choose to ignore them when they are sat in plain sight?

How can we give them hope that their lives can change
That things won't always be the same
That one day they can get off the streets and, in time
Have a place where they feel safe and have a brighter life like mine.

Phoebe Baldwin (11)
Downend School, Downend

What's Wrong With The Wind?

All I can see are kites and trees,
Distantly swaying in the breeze,
Smiles and laughter are all I can see,
Lighting up children's little faces with glee,
What a shame this cannot be a reality,
No pollution or smoke in the air scarring us
Physically and mentally.
Why can't we look after the beautiful world we were given?
Shouldn't this place be happiness and love driven?
So be aware, when you use your car
Or even dare to damage your lungs by smoke,
You could cycle in the fresh air and persuade men and
women
Of this world, to not neglect the passing wind,
Dragging the leaves by.

Olivia Johnson (11)
Downend School, Downend

Being Me

No escaping the voice in my head,
always there, even in my dreams.
Like superglue stuck to me,
it will never come off.

Distracting me from my daily life,
heart racing and sweating palms.
Stomach in knots that I can't untie.

Attacks you, takes control,
makes me want to do things I don't want to do,
bullying me, making me different.

Everyday life is ten times harder,
people don't understand,
they think it's something I choose to do.
I will never forgive it for what it does,
I will just be strong and try to be me.

Evie Williams (11)
Downend School, Downend

Family

Family are the people in your heart.
The ones that are there for you,
Wherever you are.
They will always be there,
In your heart.

Family are the people in your heart
And the ones you make memories with,
Memories you'll never forget.
Inside your heart, there they are,
Loving you and caring for you.
You love them back and care for them too.

Family are the people in your heart,
The ones that are always in your heart,
From the start until the end.
Wherever they really are,
They are always in your heart.

Chloe Hopkins (11)
Downend School, Downend

Views

My view is
The world is a whizz
And what matters to me
Is my family.
I like video games
I don't like being called names
I enjoy animations
I watch my creations.
Basil my pup is cute
He is like my precious loot.
I like the taste of cheese
I also like peas.
I build a lot of Lego
Impressive things make me go woah!
I think racism is bad
It makes me go mad.
Everyone is equal
We are just a bunch of people.
Bullying should be stopped
And at the moment it is not!

These are my views!

Jacob Lee Rothwell (12)
Downend School, Downend

Basketball

B ouncing down the court with no one in my way,

A nd scoring three-pointers with every shot,

S core after score after score the crowd goes crazy,

K een to win,

E uroLeague that's what we're about to win,

T he end of the 4th quarter is near,

B ounce, bounce, bounce goes the ball,

A ll my family there watching me about to score the winner,

L osers shout the opponent's fans as I miss the shot,

L osers, losers, losers!

Dan Adams (13)

Downend School, Downend

Drugs Are Bad

D rugs are bad and this is why
R ips apart families and friends
U nnoticed by some, but not by all
G radually starts to break you down
S uddenly, you're hooked with no way back

A ddiction is a terrible thing
R elying on drugs to get you through the day
E very day is a constant battle

B e brave and get the help you need
A lways know there are people who care
D rugs are bad and that is why.

Jacob Milsom (12)
Downend School, Downend

Technology

Car stopping,
Jaw dropping,
Technology.

Mind racing,
Lifesaving,
Technology.

Phone buzzing,
Message collecting,
Technology.

Blue screens flashing,
Emails stockpiling,
Technology.

Images blurring,
Music blaring,
Technology.

Monitors glaring,
Keyboards chattering,
Technology.

Life-enhancing,
Knowledge gathering,
Sense stimulating,
Brain inspiring,
Technology.

Lewis Jefferies (12)
Downend School, Downend

Golf

Life is like a round of golf,
With so many twists and turns,
Big hits, small hits to get to the green
Give thanks that you can play,
For the round is too short,
To let it slip away,
Because the most important shot is the next one
A round alone or with my dad
There's no telling when it will end,
In the fairway or the rough,
I will be there,
So if you can't find me, don't look long,
Check the course because that's where I belong.

Joseph Adams (13)
Downend School, Downend

The Tree On Top Of The Hill

I don't like being lonely
I don't like it at all
I don't like having to see everyone else
So happy
I bet that they aren't lonely
They say I'm lucky
Lucky to have such a beautiful view
I don't know about that
I have no one to talk to
No one by my side
Loneliness is such a bitter emotion
I know, as it is what I feel
It's a lonely life
Being the tree at the top of a hill.

Lily Seren Reynolds (12)
Downend School, Downend

Rain

Rain, rain, rain,
It falls from the sky as nature's shower,
We are all dragged into its merciless power,
It drips off our hair,
Drenches our clothes,
We all get our fair share,
Rain, rain, rain.

Puddles stand in our way,
While children laugh and play,
Rain flowing down drains,
But can cause laughter or pain,
Rain is everywhere,
Like it or not, rain is here to stay,
Rain, rain, rain.

Ellen Rebecca Roberts (11)

Downend School, Downend

Love Life

Families are sweet
Friends are the best
Bullies are wrong
You are who you are

Break down the barriers
Destroy the walls
Don't pick a fight with anyone
You are who you are

You have a good home
You have a good life
You have all you need
You are who you are

Live your life through
Enjoying every moment
Never fall down
You are who you are

Samantha Webster (12)
Downend School, Downend

I Miss My Grandad

I know you suffered,
Now it's my turn to suffer,
Now that you're gone I am broken,
There was still a new chapter in my life,

You were there for a long time,
But not for long enough,
We had good times and bad,
But now it's terrible,

I know I'm not perfect,
I know I'll never be,
I just hope you're up there,
And that you're proud of me.

Summermay Johnson (12)
Downend School, Downend

Save Our Planet

Gorillas in the trees suddenly fall,
Tigers in the distance do not stand tall,
Animals run away in fright,
Please don't kill any more tonight.
Guns and arrows, their weapons of choice,
Stand up to the hunters, give animals a voice!
Endangered species struggling to live,
Animals we are privileged to share the planet with,
Please don't hunt them or there will be no more!

Hannah Hill (11)
Downend School, Downend

Black Rose

Upon the flowers,
Upon the fields,
Lay a black rose,

And as I grew near,
I will be upon fear,
Of death and sorrow,
And shed a tear.

For those who mourn by the flowers,
Lost a bit of life,
Lost love and hope,
I shall say a prayer for those who have to cope,

All hope is gone,
The power of the black rose,
Will carry one.

Lauren James-Summersfield (12)
Downend School, Downend

My Greatest Fear

How did my greatest fears go from heights,
Bugs and killers in wardrobes

To footsteps outside my bedroom door,
Unexpected calls,
Talking to people,
Buying things in stores,
Failing in school,
Phones and messages,
Eating in front of people,
Laughter behind my back?

How did my greatest fear become my own mind?

Chloe Britton (14)
Downend School, Downend

My Dog Is The Best

My dog is the best
She is so cute
She sometimes makes a mess
But I know she's sorry

She likes running in the park
And chewing her toys
She gets excited when I see her
Makes me happy when I'm sad

My dog is the best
She has brown fur
And cute eyes
She isn't that big
But she is still the best.

Emily Kocinski (11)
Downend School, Downend

The Life

Once a man said,
"God shouldn't change people's fates,
It's their choice,
How they live
And what they say."

A woman cried and asked,
"Why does God get to pick
Who lives and who dies
Every day?"

We should all live to a point
When we're all grey and old.

Krisztian Stadinger (14)
Downend School, Downend

School's Hard

S chool is hard
C ricket is fun
H ard work I don't like
O bey, we must
O wning positives for things we do
L ate for school
S adly

H ard to get out of bed
A nd
R ushing to get down for breakfast
D yslexia sucks!

Joseph Smith (12)
Downend School, Downend

Holidays

Holidays are my thing,
As well as eating a chicken wing.
I love spending time with my family,
We can go swimming or do sports, finally.
I enjoy going to America,
But I wish I could travel to Africa.
We can explore together,
In the beautiful weather,
Holidays are my thing.

Hugo Williams (11)
Downend School, Downend

Animals

I love animals,
They're cuddly and sweet.
Just like a treat,
Many animals have little freedom
And sometimes get beaten
But together we can stop that
And help them get the freedom they need.
Are you convinced to do the good deed?

Lily Fincken (12)
Downend School, Downend

The Tiger And The Trigger

The tiger, a majestic animal
a flash in the green,
watched by a barrel and a trigger.
Its sunset-orange pelt cut and preened,
sold to the highest bidder.

The tiger, the fiery amber in its eyes faded,
the pride is broken, its face is torn and withered.
All because of something that we created
a blunt instrument, a barrel and a trigger.

We destroy our pure world; life we take
and death we deliver.
And you, yes you, what do you do?
You litter without thinking or caring
not willing to raise a finger.

Not willing to fight against something
that's a disease, something much bigger.
So at the end of the day
you did it too, you did, you pulled that trigger.

Cian Estabrook (16)
Fairfield High School, Horfield

What Do You See In Me?

I'm black, you're white and they're mixed race,
I'm mixed race, you're black and they're white,
I'm white, you're mixed race and they're black,
But does it matter what colour we are?

Yes, I may be black, white, mixed race,
Asian, American, Indian, I might be from all over the world
But just because I'm different from you
Doesn't mean I always have to be in the blue.

Yes, I'm different and that's what I want you to see
I don't wear tight jeans,
I don't wear high heels,
I don't wear tight skirts,
I don't mind being weird, crazy or stupid
Because it doesn't hurt.

So what if I'm black and you're white,
So what if I come from the other side of the world to you,
Because really, you have no clue,
It's alright for two women to be together,
It's alright for two men to be together,
It doesn't matter if you have a different religion to me,
You can be Christian, Muslim, Buddhist, Hindu,
Sikh or Jewish
But what's not alright is for you not to be you.

You can be anything you want to be
Anything in the world
You can be a dancer, singer, lawyer, doctor,
Teacher or engineer,
Electrician, coach, footballer, gymnast, male or female
It doesn't matter,
You can be gay or lesbian
But never let people judge you for who you are.

For years now people have looked at me and gone -
They're black, oh, they're white,
No, I'm not black or white, I am me,
The person who you should really see.
The person underneath this body is me
I'm not who you see on the outside, I'm on the inside
And that's what you should see in me.

Maya Lexie Sandiford (12)
Fairfield High School, Horfield

Until We Meet Again

It's been a while since you came this close
Every step you take towards me feels like air
Being taken away from my lungs
I want to get away
I want to step back
But I can't.

Your demons ignite, making me feel afraid
But it hasn't been that long since you told me
You made a mistake.
Every step you make towards me feels like a
Match burning out
And you hope there's a possibility that it'll re-alight.

But I do not want to
I want to get away
I want to step back
But I can't.

My demons attract yours
And that's why you want to attack.
It fuels your anger
It fuels your love
But it doesn't give me a sense of warmth
It scares me.

Feeling your breath on the back of my neck
Paralyses me

Making it hard to move
Making it hard to leave
Stop.

Your hands gently touching my skin
Making me think I'll be protected
Making me think that I'm safe
I really thought I was
But every time you got closer the fear grew
And every time you left
I could feel my breath coming back
From short gasps to calm and steady breaths
And I have the sense that I'll be okay

I guess until we meet again.

Weronika Kuzniewska (16)
Fairfield High School, Horfield

Mother Nature

Nature, Mother Nature
What could be greater
Fire like leaves fall in autumn
In spring mass flowers blossom
The soft whistle of the wind in summer
The flowers and leaves in full colour.

Birds sing and cry
Only to realise winter has come by
People are bitter
As they discover, it's winter
Cold and muddy is the weather
People are moody and in a bother.

At night you can still see the world of nature
The moon gleams and glistens
As if it's protecting you from danger.
The beautiful bright blue sea
Some people say the sea knows
What you can become to be
Some even say the sea knows how you feel
Which might be its best appeal.

Most of nature is now destroyed
Because of humans getting annoyed.
Annoyed, of trees in the way some get chopped for money

Some people don't see how destroying nature
Will affect our lives, it means we'll have to say goodbye
To things, we might not have considered highly prized.

Yasmin (16)
Fairfield High School, Horfield

The Lighthouse

I may live to be one hundred,
But I've already begun to shape my future.
This is a thought that has plundered
My waking moments for a while,
I know that any slip-up could tip up
The delicately weighted scales of the time after now.

There's a rock,
I cling to it.
I take to it as a gull takes to the wind, a barnacle
And I won't let go, I won't drown
Won't be drawn down,
Homework, a sack of rocks around
My ankle because she is there,
In my mind's eye, a lighthouse in the waves.

I have only to close my eyes and in the red behind my
eyelids,
Between scattered notes, fishing boats
All that's afloat in my brain,
The lighthouse appears.
The day she brings is yellow as honey wax
And soft as cinders
She runs fingers through my hair
Pulls a salt breeze through the air
She towers above me with the power and might
Of the brightest star in the darkest night

A raging bull's delight
The future is my light.

Lola Hambrook (16)
Fairfield High School, Horfield

4329

My name is candidate number 4329
I got to a school called centre number 51521
My best friend is anything above sixty-five percent,
My hobby is doing hours of revision a day,

I live on a spreadsheet at least
Ninety-five per cent of the time,
I am passionate about remembering
Terabytes of data at once,
My dream is to one day move along for the next batch,
My legacy is twenty papers to mark.

I promise that I am more.

I am more than just a number,
I do more than encumber,

I dream of travelling the Earth,
I dream of writing tales,
I have seen death and birth,
I am so scared that I'll fail.

I have so many traits
But school dictates
That I am just another weight,
Another thing on their plate.

I am not dull,
Like a flame, I shine,
And my name is not 4329.

Evan Davies (15)
Fairfield High School, Horfield

Peace

Peace appears to speak in shattered puzzle pieces,
Scattered carelessly amongst broken bones and silent souls,
Hidden artfully in the back of sinful minds and praying
hearts,
That long for a time where man-caused combat, warfare,
conflict ceases.

The strength to save this world we litter
With bullets and bitter screams
From dagger rips in skin's seams,
Lies in these pieces,

Pieces of a bigger picture, overshadowed by ignorance
And heartless bloodshed.
Don't risk countless, cataclysmic, calamitous years
Of weapon conducted conversations,
Instead of discarding pride and picking up peace.

Deborah Omolegan-Obe (14)
Fairfield High School, Horfield

'Perfect' Pictures

Hours upon hours,
Watching YouTube, Netflix.
Scrolling through Instagram,
Seeing 'perfect' pictures.

Streaks on Snapchat,
Every day.
New episodes on Netflix,
Every week.

Gotta watch the new video,
Go like their new post.
Have to post the best pictures of myself.

Back at school,
What is that?
A new series on Netflix,
Haven't watched that yet.

Hours upon hours,
Watching YouTube, Netflix.
Scrolling through Instagram,
Seeing 'perfect' pictures.

Tilly Spencer (16)
Fairfield High School, Horfield

Panic

Running from the feeling of disappointment,
the knowing that this isn't going to be the last time,
the last time you can't breathe,
move or talk,
the last time you hear voices,
getting louder and louder as you try,
try to ignore them,
her mind is a prison,
that wants to be forgiven,
but no, its a repetition,
louder and louder,
it will surround her,
until she can take no more.
No more she says,
but this won't be the last time.

Eve Shobbrook (12)
Fairfield High School, Horfield

Racism

R eality of society
A ll becomes clear
C hildren being treated differently
I t's all because of their skin colour
S omething they cannot choose
M ay everyone be equal.

Admas Combley (13)

Fairfield High School, Horfield

Nothing

Emptiness, nothingness
Rich people need me
Poor people have me
But everyone knows my name

I'm just like a blank space
I need to be filled
My heart is empty
My heart is chilled

Everyone knows my name
The love I have is none
The bad spirits I bring
People's happiness is gone

I am a see-through ghost
No one knows I'm there
But everyone has the feeling
When their feelings bare

That's who I am
Nothingness
An empty, black abyss
A cold-hearted spirit
That no one will miss

Emptiness, nothingness
I have nothing to hold

When you have me
You act different, you act boldly

Some people need me
Some people want me
The shock I may have
The lives I may change

That's who I am
My name is Nothingness
A cold-hearted abyss
That no one will miss.

But there is another side to me
There are people on the streets
They have nothing
But their community comes together

People make friends
People laugh, people cry
People scream, people shout
People stay friends for life.

People make friends,
Who turn quite close
Some people become family
Some people know them the most.

That's who I am
Nothingness

A two-sided spirit
That some people won't miss.

Harleigh Bradwell (12)
King Edward VI Community College, Totnes

Lost Souls

Listen, they're singing through the trees
Watch their dancing through the leaves
Voices, voices screaming,
"Will you help me?"
Wandering the world, longing to be free

Chains of despair weighing them down
Seeking solitude from town to town
Innocents trapped in a tortuous cycle
Victims of unfair trials

Living in and amongst shadows
Forever burdened by their sorrows
Animals and children run away
Adults dismiss them as is their way

Troubled teens bullied and beaten
Adults sad and weakened
People who couldn't handle their problems
Who took their lives due to racism

Listen, listen don't ignore their song
People say, "Listen or soon they'll be gone"
So don't ignore them
You have an imagination, let them in,
You don't know, they could be your kin.

Beth Wallis (14)
King Edward VI Community College, Totnes

A Bird, The Tree And The Sky

A brittle bird sat in the tree
He wanted to be, he wanted to be
Up in the sky, with all the best
Perched on a cloud to have a rest

A thoughtful bird sat on a cloud
Missing home, missing home
So he flew back down till he could see
All his family sat in the tree

A happy bird settled in the tree
Loving life till the eye could see
Then the bark started to snap
Soon he realised it was a trap

A startled bird sat trapped in the tree
Trying to see, trying to see
Then his mum flew right down
And slowly drifted over the town

A mother bird flew around
Trying to save the bird from bound
Then she flew back from town
To help the bird get down

A saved bird out of the tree
As happy as could be

He and his family flew up into the sky
To test if he could still fly.

Kyle Daniel (12)
King Edward VI Community College, Totnes

The Pattern

What goes on inside your head,
Filled with knowledge of old,
And with intelligence, it is fed,
Where imagination falls like rain,
But inside behold a prison of red and blue,
Your brain catches you in never-ending thought,
Escape from the madness,
Come into the light
Back to the relaxation of an empty mind,
And the power of thought,
Your mentality is covered in the colours of imagination
Reds, greens, yellows and blues,
Drip slowly down the pages of your mind
To form a pattern,
The pattern of your life, your memories
And it is not complete
There are gaps in the trail
Yet to be filled with bright brilliance
Finish the pattern, finish your life.

Harry Green (12)
King Edward VI Community College, Totnes

More Than Nothing

Ice caps melting,
Polar bears dying,
But we do nothing,
While sitting in our warm, fast cars.

Plastic floating upon the oceans,
Turtles trapped and choking,
But we do nothing,
While we drink sweet, fizzy drinks.

Trees are crashing to the ground,
But we don't hear a sound,
Treetop toucans and orangutans,
Are forced to leave their homes.

Snow is falling,
Seagulls calling,
Just begging to be let in,
But we do nothing,
While writing poems,
In our warm English class.

It's not their fault,
They can't change it,
It's up to us to help them,
So why do we do nothing?

Hannah Wintle (12)
King Edward VI Community College, Totnes

Floating

Floating.
Water surrounding, encompassing, enclosing
Me and extreme masses of other.
Floating endlessly forever,
Never ever biodegrading.
A hundred years is all it's been;
All this damage just in time.
We kill, we murder,
We destroy -
They eat; we kill.
We are polluting in our millions.
We spread diseases and viruses.
The seas are emptying.

You can vanquish us,
You can collectively rid this world of this plague.
Awareness has been raised.
The ideas are changing.
Hope is in our sights.
You can still win this war -
The future is not yet written.

Isak Williams (12)
King Edward VI Community College, Totnes

Universe

The wide empty void not yet explored,
The not yet understood place,
Just go up and up,
Taller than us,
Taller than a giraffe,
The technical rocket flying far away,
But now because of the zooming cars and flying planes,
That is all getting demolished by us,
Greenhouse gases from cars, planes and trains.
Burning a towering hole in the atmosphere,
Just why can't we go back to the olden days?
With horse and carriage zooming past.
The universe is as easy to damage as a human body,
Like you and me,
But do you really want the green, as green can be,
Earth to demolish slowly?

Charlotte Lewis (12)
King Edward VI Community College, Totnes

Life Or Death?

When we come to life,
We think of nothing more.
Nothing more than what will happen,
Will we live or die?

People think of Heaven and Hell,
But is it really true?
The more we grow, the more we think
What will happen when death comes our way?

As we get older,
The thoughts become bolder,
What can we do?
Will all become blue?

Nobody knows how long they will live,
Sometimes we wonder about falling off a cliff.
We could die any minute,
This could be us finished...

Alana Pope (11)
King Edward VI Community College, Totnes

War

We wake up and we think
Who should I be today?
We only listen to the words of others
Because we are hit with a fear
But we should listen to our mothers.
They tell us to
'Ignore their lies'
But they should know that would happen,
When you see a pig that flies.
We should be proud of our own skin and others will follow
Because others will not feel so hollow,
You will feel alive yourself again,
There will be no more pain.

Kloé Potter (12)
King Edward VI Community College, Totnes

Haunted House

My heart is pounding in my chest,
The spooky spirits have found me on my quest.
I'm running at the speed of light,
And all this darkness never seemed so bright.
My claustrophobia is kicking in,
But no one knows what lies within.
I hear the clock ticking, *tick, tick, tick,*
And all of a sudden, a mighty kick.
I run as fast as I can at my top speed,
And all I feel is a frosty breeze...

George Mathys (11)
King Edward VI Community College, Totnes

Deep In The Woods

Deep in the wood
Where no one stood
The wind would howl
Almost like a growl
You can hear footsteps echo through the wood
I'm standing here under my hood
I'm surrounded in feelings in my head
Is it what people have said
No one knows
I'm standing here all alone
Scared and cold
The growls seem real
Nights drawing in
Deep in the wood
Where no one stood.

Sasha Barrett (12)
King Edward VI Community College, Totnes

Ocean Shore

The soft sand encases my feet
Waves punching the shore

My anxiety writes itself in the sand
My thoughts fade away

Starfish sunbathe on the shore;
Sea lapping up the sand

The blue ocean air; fresh and salty

Hermit crabs hunch up in their houses

The shores wave to each other

The sun is shining on me
A smile beams across his face.

Emily May (12)
King Edward VI Community College, Totnes

Pollution

Cars and vans whizzing around,
And fumes all in the air,
Rubbish being chucked around,
Making animals all dead.

If this never stops,
Then our world is gone,
Lifeless unlike it was,
Once before.

Eve Widger (11)
King Edward VI Community College, Totnes

All You Can Do Is Your Best

I don't want to seem like I'm complaining,
But there's just something I feel like saying.
Just something I feel that I'd like to mention,
And my one and only intention,
Is to attempt to help cause the prevention,
Of this annoying issue, so please pay attention.
It's something I find most people do,
I bet you sometimes do too.
I know what you're thinking... *why don't you tell us*
What's got you in such a fuss?
Well, now I'll tell you exactly what,
I'll tell you everything I've got.
What annoys me is that so many people,
Give up and don't try at all.
They simply say that 'it's too problematic',
They won't attempt any sum in mathematics,
Or anything else at all.
For example, when I'm at school,
The teachers say, "Have a go,"
But a lot of students just say, "No."
Is it because they just don't want to?
Because it's something they can't be bothered to do?
I do think that's sometimes the case,
But there's another reason I can trace.
Maybe lots of people give up because of fear,
The more I think about it, the more it seems clear.

Everyone is afraid of failure,
They're worried about what will happen later.
They think that if they try, there's nothing they will gain,
They'll just end up failing and feeling pain.

Well, I don't mean to whine,
But you're not going to win every time.
Everyone fails and makes mistakes,
And when you do it's bound to ache.
But if you get up and try again,
It's bound to pay off in the end.
It's better to have a go,
Even if you might not have won by tomorrow.
You'll achieve something eventually,
So just keep trying and be the best you can be.
So don't get worried, don't get stressed,
Because all you can do is your best.

Lauren Hamilton (12)
Nailsea School, Nailsea

I'm Sorry - Spoken Poetry

I'm sorry that I'm not beautiful
Because my eyes are not blue and my hair is not blonde,
But trust me, I'm sorry,
I'm sorry that I don't ruin my skin
By putting a pound of make-up on my face every morning.
I'm sorry that I don't wake up at four in the morning
To curl my hair so I can come to school looking like a
princess,
I'm sorry that I don't look like the girl on the front page of
your magazine,
You know the one where they are photoshopped to look like
an alien.
Where not a bone in their body is too big or too small
Because they're perfect,
They're who you look up to,
When I'm older I'm going to make a magazine of true
beauty,
A magazine where girls can feel loved
Where there is no fakeness, no plastic and no photoshop,
Maybe then the world will be better,
Maybe then boys will realise that nobody actually looks like
that.
Nobody wakes up, rolls out of bed and can just be perfect,
But does it really matter as long as you are you?
But I'm really sorry for trying and blunting myself,

Ruining my self-esteem
Because when I get home from school and take off my make-up
And undo my hair,
I can't even look in the mirror,
I can't face it.
What I truly look like.

Lily May Bartle-Jenkins (13)
Nailsea School, Nailsea

Freedom Fighters

Running through the scorching sun.
Chanting under their breaths.
Their souls holding tight to reality,
Sweat pouring down their black skin.

The days run on, the nights grow cold.
Constantly moving, constantly being chased.
Holding on to a thin thread of hope.
Far away from their captured home.

As the landscape changes around them,
As the seasons come and go.
They're still running onwards.
Still holding on, never letting go.

As they lay asleep at night.
They dream of one thing, forever on their mind.
To be with their families: children, husbands and wives.
To stop running from their old captured life.

Still, nightmares run through their dreams sometimes.
The black smoky horses with their trails of coal.
The chains clanking, the stars growing dark.
The torture never ending.

Sometimes as they wake up screaming in the dark.
They'll wonder if they'll ever escape their old path.

Wonder if there is no way to escape.
Wonder if this is just their only fate.

This is why we need to take hold.
Capture our dreams and be ever so bold.
Fight for these people, these freedom fighters.
Don't let the colour of their skin set them apart.

Maria Dodd (12)
Parkstone Grammar School, Poole

The Storm

He resembled snow,
Falling silently into our lives,
Clouding your vision as the blizzard he was
You couldn't see anything
You couldn't see us
And with your hat, scarf and gloves,
Though you looked warm and safe,
You could barely breathe...

The snow became incessant,
Our garden, your street, even in our home,
Everything was frozen,
Hidden and chained down.

The worst part,
Was how the cold embraced you,
Leaving you with no memory of our warm sun,
And though we kept inviting you back,
We became just a small part of your glistening white mind.

Eventually, you caught frostbite,
Trapped in his jaws,
But you noticed our rays of light shining through,
You held onto them as we melted the snow together,

I know the brightness hurts your eyes,
But you yourself are too bright

To be hidden
Under any white blanket.

A season later, the storm passed,
And we all moved into spring.

I know some places are still melting,
Some are frozen solid;
Just remember my sun will always be behind your clouds,
No matter what nature throws at you.

Olivia Girling (16)
Parkstone Grammar School, Poole

Why?

I'm fourteen and insecure
Do you want to know why I'm insecure?
No, it's not because I think I'm fat or ugly
I'm insecure because I have a ridiculous fear
I don't want males near me
It shouldn't be real and yet it is
And the only one to blame is him

I was ten, young and naive
He was fifteen
He was loud and brash
I was quiet and trusting
I trusted him
I knew he would never hurt me
But then he asked and I was confused
He asked again a few days later
I declined again but his convincing was greater
I didn't want to but he was scary
I saw how he acted with his brother
I didn't want to be another.

It happened a few times, each time much worse
All his words became even more perverse
I started protecting myself,
Wearing more layers
Eventually, I stopped going altogether
My family was concerned

But they never asked
So I never told
It wasn't until many months later that I broke
A cold November night, in tears I awoke
I went to my sister and mother and spilled the whole story,
Even to this day, they're filled with guilt
Wishing that they'd reached out...

The police were called, but nothing happened
He got a slap on the wrist, but me?
What did I get?
Sleepless nights, years of therapy
A fear that I shouldn't exist
I shouldn't get uncomfortable when a boy comes near me
I shouldn't stay away because I fear them
Even to this day, I have my doubts
Because I pushed it so far down where it couldn't get out
But why would I make up such a thing?
To make myself suffer from nothing?

Four years later and I'm starting therapy again
I thought it was over but it's come back
It's affecting my life even more
I can't form relationships because I'm so insecure
Why do I have to be broken?
Why did he have to take advantage of me?
I was only ten, he was fifteen!

Max Downey (15)
Riverside Centre EOTAS, Swindon

We Are Society

On a daily basis, we all tend to blame society for our
problems
When in actuality, we can only blame ourselves;
We are Society.
So when your future kid says 'I want a nose job'
And your response is something along the lines of
'No you don't, it's just that we live in a judgemental society'
And continue to say they should love themselves
However when you take them to school,
And you make a comment on someone's appearance -
'Living with a nose that big must be hell!'
You are subconsciously taking part in this judgemental
society,
That you told your child not to worry about,
While still continuing to tell them to love themselves.

Brooke Harmsworth-Shand (15)

Riverside Centre EOTAS, Swindon

My Love, The Moon

I'm in a trance
My eyes are fixed to the bright haze of the moon above
Such beauty in the pitch-black sky
He has caught me breathless
I try to break my sight but I can't
For the moon feels just like I do
So lonely
Stuck within the sky full of stars

I'm in a daze
Engulfed within the bright embrace of his stare
Ghostly whisper say their goodbye
As for the sun must rise
So old and wise
I will see you another time

I'm breaking free
Free from his spell
Goodbye my love
I wish you well
Now your performance has come and gone
Time for the spotlight to be thy sun
Now please my love,
Be gone.

Ash Clarke (15)
Riverside Centre EOTAS, Swindon

Memories Flood

Memories flood
Sparkle is lost, the pain is showing,
Without him even knowing.
Plenty of love but she chooses to inject a death catcher.
A death catcher made of venom
With the witness of her flesh and blood
Her son, her son that adores her, she could do no wrong
Tears falling...

Memories flood
His anger boils and he's now evil
Unloved and pushed away
Venom came first
And now a simple 'please or thank you'
Doesn't escape from his way
The soul snatched ruined him
Her choices betrayed him

Tears still falling.
The killer of the family spirit.
The drugs have won...

Leah Harding (16)
Riverside Centre EOTAS, Swindon

The Darkness Inside

Depression
The darkness that lurks behind you
Waiting for you to break and surrender yourself
To its twisted game of horrors
Where he follows you, poking and prodding you
With the harshness of the world...

Then he brings you gifts of anxiety
The fear of the population and the unknown
The sudden rapid pulsating of the heart
Begging for a gasp of oxygen
From the spawn of the world.

Then the loss of emotion strides on in
Giving you the sense of emptiness
Leaving you as a hollow shell
Bound by the pressures of the world...

Sammy Hawkins (14)
Riverside Centre EOTAS, Swindon

Speak Out Loud

You can change everything
Speak out loud
You can change everything
Do yourself proud

Put the past behind
It's now or never
Together we can be kind
We can change it forever

Hidden behind a fake smile
Open your eyes and see
Hidden behind a fake smile
The sadness beneath me

Nightmares become reality
Tears rolling down my face
My broken soul empty
I have lost my place

Self-esteem has gone
Drowning in thoughts
Self-esteem has gone
I am now distraught

They will not defeat me
I will stand up

You can't bully me
I won't give up.

Ellie Morgan (14)
Riverside Centre EOTAS, Swindon

Escaping My Nightmares

I just can't seem to escape my thoughts
My thoughts are the only weapon in the war against reality
I can't escape the chain of my nightmares
That are created by my memories
The nightmares that unfold in my mind
Wrap their evil hands around my soul
The sweat pours down my cheeks as if I have stage fright
I awaken out of my sleep and urgently turn on my light
The dark nightmares may follow me
But they'll never win the fight.

Faith Taylor (16)
Riverside Centre EOTAS, Swindon

Lost

He was like a brother,
A brother to me,
I told him all my secrets,
We would have the best time,
Playing for hours on end,
Riding bikes,
Skating on our penny boards,
Playing football,
Running for hours on end in the woods,
I want to see my best friend,
Not just his name engraved in stone,
The words will haunt me forever,
10th of June 2015
I am lost,
All alone...

Callum Smart (14)
Riverside Centre EOTAS, Swindon

Discrimination

Anxious, tired and depressed,
you would not expect this, but I was stressed
you may ask, why is this so?
A fourteen-year-old boy who felt so low.
My name is Leon Watts and I was bullied.

Every morning my mind was racing like V12 engine
my heart beating like a drum
pounding blood surged through my head
my lungs full of panic
before the day had begun.

Leon Watts (14)
Riverside Centre EOTAS, Swindon

One World

Break the silence,
Break the silence,
Shout out loud!

Tell the teacher,
Tell the teacher,
Don't follow the crowd!

Dry your tears,
Dry your tears,
Speak out loud!

Stop the bullies,
Stop the bullies,
End it now!

Change the outcome,
Change the outcome,
Make our world one!

Bethany Hannah Michelle Bradbury-Newton (14)
Riverside Centre EOTAS, Swindon

Space

Dark is the night in space
Where up and down are relative
Light shines around the planet
And there is a fight to see it.
There is a blight on the scorched planet below
But the type is unknown,
Just like the sky is the planet below.

Isaac Condé Dilley (15)
Riverside Centre EOTAS, Swindon

The Hunt

The rider stands tall over his army of psychopaths
Waiting eagerly for the murder spree to start
A smile crawls over his face as he imagines the terror, the
blood, the thrill

The empty hounds barked and snarled,
Their thoughtless minds as they caught the scent of yet
another innocent soul
The hunt was on

The mindless army tore through the woods
The rider and his terror-stricken horse galloped after them
The murderous rider's cruel laugh echoed through the
woods, blanketing it with a layer of dread

The fox caught the scent of the mad hounds
A shiver of terror shot through him
He was momentarily paralysed
The fox ran
He turned and twisted but wherever he ran the fox could
not escape the screams of the empty hounds

Louder now, closer now, faster now, too late now
The psychopaths were on him
The last thing he saw as they ripped him apart was the
excitement in the rider's eyes.

Belle Taylor (12)
Sands School, Ashburton

Arthritis

Zoom in to the world and into one house, Totnes
Zoom in more to a small room on the second floor and
watch
3... 2... 1... and she's awake
She is writhing around, trying to stop the pain
But the more she moves, the more she wakes
The more she wakes, the more she is aware of the pain

This goes on for 15 minutes
She cries out
Cut to the morning. That girl was me
The morning stiffness and falling out of bed to get up in the
morning
Grudgingly getting ready for a long, tedious day

During the day the pain gets worse, the stiffness intensifies
Take a painkiller, sit down, move about, repeat
Falling asleep on the bus home
Staying awake to avoid the pain
Laying in bed waiting for the cycle to start again

The month goes by
And then the 25th I go to the hospital
To a second family
The routine of the day starts, check up, cannula in, and
waiting for the tests to come back and sitting
I walked in at 11:00 and here we are, it's 3
Still waiting for medicine

Every month the same routine
Every month the same wait
Every day the same pain
Every day the same fatigue
Friends that want to help
But just don't understand
Family helping with their own remedies
Doctors' broken promises.

All these things crowd my head
Spinning around my head and
I break!

Mae Rose Webster (13)
Sands School, Ashburton

If All Was Lost

Boom! sounded the cannons as they rounded up the men
"March and fire!" shouted the sergeant as they cleared up
the wire
All the sergeant could see was blood, mud and mist

"Quiet little Kevin or go back to camp!"
Kevin stayed at camp and lay in bed
Trying to get the bad thoughts out of his head
He sat there lonely, wishing for his only pony

The sun rose higher
Clearing the mist and creating a warm fire
His father was wishing to see his son again
He hopes to go fishing yet the war split them apart
Kevin was being taken in the back of a van
They were being shaken

They were tattered and tortured as they laid there
defenceless
Skinny and ripped every time they ran, they tripped

All the lives lost and the families that trembled
But don't worry, we will always remember.

Finlay Hawkins (13)
Sands School, Ashburton

World War II

Oh, Hitler got his army and marched into France,
While there was much bloodshed,
The Germans would advance.
Now time for Hitler to break the Polish corridor
As they marched in, they thought themselves a warrior.

Stalin helped,
The Polish yelped
And Poland was defeated.

Now let's not forget about Italy,
They wanted more than just Sicily.
So the Italians invaded,
Some place with wooden spears
And the Italians continued
To blast off their rears.

Wait, let's go back to Stalin
Who got a knife in his back
Because Hitler decided to attack!

Vincent Byrne (12)
Sands School, Ashburton

Cruel

As the dodo continued to prance,
The man threw his lance,
It was too late,
The dodo did not even have time to glance.

As the pet snake was flushed down the loo,
In all the gross goo,
It was then that he knew,
That he was no longer loved.

"Don't go in the slaughterhouse!"
Were the wise words spoken to the cow by the mouse,
"Don't be silly, I'm not a moron,
It'll never lead to me being gone!"
The mouse began to cry
As he saw his friend die.
It was simply cruel.

Ben Martin (12)
Sands School, Ashburton

Homelessness

Homeless should end
Some people are rich, some are poor
Everyone deserves a friend
Someone to open the door

Why do the rich turn on the homeless?
When they have so little
When people are unkind it causes a mess
It makes self-worth feel brittle

If all the rich would just give a penny
It would make a difference
Rich people have so many
Why can't people have common sense?

I am against homelessness
I am against hopelessness.

Poppy Pugh (12)
Sands School, Ashburton

Mental Health

Some days I wake up and I don't like what I see,
It's not that I think I'm fat or ugly,
It's more than that.
It's as if I don't even like being me.
I've been made to feel so small by society,
That I have now taken to suffering silently,
Because as humans we are quiet,
We don't talk about feelings which
Does more harm than good.
You end up battling everything inside,
People have no idea about all the hurt and pain I hide.
How I cried myself to sleep last night,
Or how I've been avoiding Skyping my best friend,
Because I don't want to show her this side.
The side where I can't keep it together,
And the most messed up part is,
I have no idea why.

It seems like nobody ever pursues their dreams,
They all just settle for the 9-5 routine.
We're all just living machines,
All programmed to the exact same thing.
Work, eat, sleep, and you start to think, *that's it.*
When in reality, you just want to break free,
And be who you always wanted to be.

So you continue to wear a mask,
Keep saying to yourself, "You're going to be okay,
If you can get through another day."
But you can't solve pain with short highs,
So you resort to late night cries.
We try to hide our feelings which is such a sad reality,
The other day I came home from school,
Comforted by my dark thoughts and just broke down,
Just cried and cried.
And then just about the next day,
Like everything was fine.

You start to think it's your fault that things
Have turned our this way.
I'm going insane.
When will it stop?
Nobody should ever deserve to live the same way,
So I force all my energy into being okay.

In every picture, I would have the biggest smile,
You wouldn't even question it.
I want to be free, living free from scrutiny,
No longer haunted by the scars on your skin
But to be proud of who you have become.
I create this character, she is perfect, she never falls.
So many people do the same thing.
Shut out our darkest thoughts and just simply live.
Ask yourself, are you living or merely existing?

But it's at that moment when you are at your lowest
You understand that it is from feeling pain,
You can finally heal,
No, it won't be easy, one day we will look back
And the words won't hurt as much anymore,
We will look back and be proud
Because it made us the person we are today.

Keala Bewick (12)
St Ives School, Higher Tregenna

Bullying

Bullying isn't right!
And taking the fun out of someone is wrong.
You and I are the same,
So why blame people for who they are,
Whether they're black, white or Asian,
We are a massive community,
That inherits the Earth together.
So, when I see people bullying someone,
For being poor or having a disability,
I don't think it's cool
But it is cruel.
It isn't right that all our ancestors will look down one day
"What are they doing with their lives,
Having wars about religion and being too greedy for
power."
And how we evolved around violence and greed,
It isn't good.
And whenever I see a bigger kid bully a smaller one, I think,
Has it all come down to this? Is this who we are?
It is our decision to choose,
It's time to choose for the future of the human race!

Logan Cording (12)
St Ives School, Higher Tregenna

When Your Friend Laughs At An Offensive Joke

You're relaxing at home,
Your phone dings,
It's one of your best friends.

You unlock your phone, grinning to yourself,
As this particular friend is the best source of your happiness.
The glue to a broken vase,
Granting hope,
And a chance of a future for this poor little vase.

The text is a picture,
A picture that sends millions of goosebumps
Scrawling up your arms,
And a sandstorm through your mind.

Although, through the cloudy skies,
You have crystal clear doubts,
Blinding any other useless thoughts.

This can't be them, you think,
Yet as you check the top of the screen,
Fear surges, flooding through your body,
Your blood icy.

For this picture,
This picture on your screen,

Could offend most of the seven billion people
On this entire earth.

Tears prick your eyes,
As the sting of betrayal boils your icy blood.
You're not mad,
You're not sad,
But you feel like...

Like this figure, you praise for their sunshine energy,
Their wild personality,
The person you trusted the most,
Is now like all the others.

You feel like you're spinning,
In a never-ending vortex,
Of all their promises...
Their smile they greet you with every morning,
Their sunshine just as grey and boring,
As the day without them.

The glue has all run out,
There is none in stock in any shop.
The vase lies there,
Unfulfilled,
Like its whole life has been cut short,
Right in front of its eyes.

The vase is ruined,
Into the bin, it goes.

Taia Christie-Beckett (12)
St Ives School, Higher Tregenna

The Truth Of My Time In Primary

One of the most important things to me
Is friends and company
When I started my new primary school
A group of girls wouldn't talk to me at all
One girl said she hated the colour of my hair.
I tried to pretend that I didn't care
When I tried to be kind
They whispered bad things about me,
When I turned my back to hide.
It had gotten worse in Year One
But my story had just begun.

I did have one friend,
But she wasn't with me until the end
She had moved schools in Year Four
The girls still bullied me, it was like I'd fallen to the floor.
I thought once I had made a friend
But I was betrayed
They put a note in my drawer,
It said horrible things about me,
I felt like my heart was scratched by a claw.

In Year Six,
I made a friend and called her Pix.
The bullies had gone away,
Hip, hip, hooray!

Now I have lots of friends
With all their weird trends
But best of all
They love it when I call!

Jamie-Mai Semmons-Waite (11)
St Ives School, Higher Tregenna

Trying Not To Break

Not so long ago
In a place closer than it really seems
There lived a silly little girl
With a world full of dreams

Tired,
Abandoned storefronts and cracked cement
Kids walking along the bridge
Wondering what would happen if they jumped.

How much longer can I take?
Constantly trying not to break
It goes on and on, day by day,
Another piece of me chiselled away.

Broken,
Cigarette smoke and muffled curse words,
Sweatpants and UGG boots with holes.

Too fat and too ugly,
Too judgemental and a fool,
She could never just be perfect,
And society is cruel.

Hypocrisy,
We tell kids not to bully one another
Yet we turn a blind eye on ones with pain inside
So palpable you could almost touch it

I want to leave, I want to go
Please let me go, oh please
Do you agree life's one big con?
Please don't look for me when I'm gone.

Kate Cann (12)
St Ives School, Higher Tregenna

Pollution

Pollution, pollution,
Will we ever have a solution?

I can spot it in the sea,
There's some over in that tree,
Do you think we will ever be free?

It makes me sick,
Seeing oil slick,
The shore black
Sad, with the blue it must lack.

And the litter pickers
Keep getting quicker
As the smog gets thicker
As the sky starts to clog.

The bags dance
As the bottles prance,
Across the swollen hills
We call a landfill.

At first glance, the sea splashes
As more plastic makes the fish turn to ashes.

And the plastic is an infection,
Constantly flooding our seas
As it spreads to the next section.

Can we save it?
Will we save it?
We will always crave it!

Archie Hart (12)

St Ives School, Higher Tregenna

I Really Love The Ocean

I really love the ocean,
The sand, the sea and the sky,
But if the birds keep eating plastic,
They will be unable to fly.

I really love the ocean,
And the way the fish swim,
But if the plastic keeps polluting,
Then the fish will end up grim.

I really love the ocean,
And the way the seaweed sways,
But if you drop that water bottle,
Then you'll ruin it in days.

I really love the ocean,
And I know you do too,
But if the world keeps polluting,
It will be impossible to undo.

I really hate the ocean,
Now I'm old and grey,
If only I could go back in time,
And they would listen to what I say.

Lukas Poprawski (12)
St Ives School, Higher Tregenna

Polluting Plastic

Gushing, spraying, tossing, turning, chopping,
Our sea is beautiful, why destroy it?
Sand, sea, shells, we enjoy it a whole lot,
This thing, killing, harming, hurting creatures,
It has one name, one very special name
It begins with 'p' - polluting plastic.

Do you really want this for where we live?
The animals of the ocean kingdom,
They were all happy, I will repeat, *they were*
This isn't just about animals,
It's about us, the next generation,
What if the magical beauty has gone?
All they will see is the word that starts with 'p',
It's called the dreadful polluting plastic.

Frankie Louise Jeffs (13)

St Ives School, Higher Tregenna

Black Or White, We Are All Equal

Black is no different from white,
White is no different to black,
For white people, freedom is like a kite,
But for black people, a smile is followed by an attack,

The way I would like to be treated is fairly,
Which in 1960 would not occur,
Black people's lives were cheated,
But for white people, they just didn't care.

For here we are in 2019,
Things still aren't perfect,
Racism is still happening,
In India, Nigeria and Kuwait.

But things can be better,
With kindness, respect and happiness,
We can all do this together,
With thoughts and friendliness.

Emily Bailie (12)
St Ives School, Higher Tregenna

Why Homework Should Be Banned

Homework should be banned,
Even a teacher said so,
But nobody will listen,
The smartest countries don't even have it though,
It's pointless and bad,
And it's wasting children's time,
Because it's making them work,
And encouraging a rhyme,
Children have better things to do,
But you don't care do you?
You assume we have all the time in the world,
But that just isn't true,
We have better things to do,
Why don't you just ban it?
It's only common sense,
You take thirty to forty hours from our week already,
It's only common sense.

Toby Bungay (12)
St Ives School, Higher Tregenna

Questions

Why live life to the dullest
and look at the world spin by?
Why watch the world switch from day to night,
just using our eyes?
How does the universe work, how do birds fly?
We need answers to these questions, here where we lie.
How did we create these horrific fights,
when the world is just a blue and green light?
When watching lights, we get hypnotic eyes,
we go to sleep and realise that everyone has rights.
You and I are one, walking under stars and lights,
we are dreaming the same big dreams -
so no need for a fight.

Keala Hamm (12)
St Ives School, Higher Tregenna

Bullying

A bully is a boy or a girl
Who makes you feel bad
Who says things or does things
That makes you feel sad.

They may think they are cool
Only because they call you names
They also might make you scared
But you shouldn't let them think
That you are going to hide.

What do you do
If you're bullied today?
You must try to stay calm,
And just walk away.

You should know
That you can talk to your teachers
Parents, family and friends
So then you can know
That the bullying will end.

Eloise May Hunt (12)
St Ives School, Higher Tregenna

What Happens If You Don't Fit In?

I have been bullied,
I know how it feels,
I don't think bullies know how it feels
Bullying can be for pleasure
Bullying can gain acceptance
Bullying can be to show off.
I felt depressed and isolated,
It's like being in a prison cell.
Control, cruelty
Or compassion and caring
Think, think how cruel you're being
We are human, we need to learn to be better.

Max Thornton (12)
St Ives School, Higher Tregenna

Sometimes

Sometimes being different is a good thing.
Sometimes all you need is a little self-confidence.
Sometimes you just need to blank out the rest of the world.
Sometimes all you need is someone who can
Look past the outside and see what is truly inside.

Kyla Collier (11)

St Ives School, Higher Tregenna

My Family

F orever in my heart.
A lways there for me.
M aking me happy.
I ncredibly smart.
L oving and caring.
Y ou will always be with me!

Wesley Veal (12)
St Ives School, Higher Tregenna

Myopia

Disdain for a fellow Luddite, as is such for a Vulgarian,
But never is it in, this dawning for our barbarian.
And as does decree, the most inane creature's devices,
A contagion of all the lackadaisical imbecile's vices!
Begins the end and so has fallen, all decree and his master's
voice,
A beginning without its end. Thus, is born ending; begin
Ruse, a woman becomes a man and a man becomes a
woman.
All end's beginning and all beginning's end, become for the
world,
Such is for a time we live.
Penniless, forgotten and derided is etiquette's last
preservation,
Decayed for sin made beauty, replaced antecedents'
reservation.
Last hopes stand-off and alone, help it become not only it's
own,
But make it for a living, take the ungiving, it won't last
alone.

George Smith-Easton (14)

Steiner Academy Exeter, Exeter

Inner Most Nervosa

Our worlds, they collide,
I have power, not control,
These feelings will never subside,
Long ago, was tainted my soul,
My addiction, it shattered my pride,
We will never coincide.

The mirrors on the wall,
Are telescopes to my flaws,
One step over and my work will fall,
Salty, bittersweet, bites my tongue raw.

At first, it was working,
I felt satisfied, I felt empty,
But then my eyes were sinking,
My lips were cracking, my nails were breaking,
My body was tiring, I felt like I was going insane.

This whole ordeal has become a routine,
But it's not routine, it's an addiction,
I'm attached to my own restriction,
It's the only thing tying me down.

I'm shivering, I'm shaking,
I tell myself it's all okay,
I'm terrified, my ankles are quaking,
I'm gagging at my sick display.

I think I'm in control,
But I'm not,
I don't control it,
It controls me,
The faded black getting darker around my eyes,
Hiding it with my painted lies.

Arms, neck, back and thighs,
Count it all and measure my sides,
Stay under a hundred or have nothing at all,
It doesn't matter what you do,
Nobody will see you fall six feet under.

Burning the fat from my thighs,
With an oversized jumper, I disguise,
The perilous addiction that will be my demise,
As my long-shed tears dry.

I'm getting steadily sicker,
My actions barely a flicker,
I'm coming to terms with it,
I don't know if I want to get better,
But I know I need to.
The hunger feels good,
How do I quit this?
These thoughts are killing me,
The numbers are controlling me.

From my rugged spinal chain,
My artist of disdain,
My tears of pureblood rain,
A skeleton is all that remains.

I feel like there's a knife at my throat,
I'm sinking lower and lower,
I just want to press it harder,
Draw blood and
Free myself,
From this innermost nervosa.

Kaya Ballantyne (14)
Steiner Academy Exeter, Exeter

Ivy

A shy cat with a shy heart,
She hides from the abusive in The Ivy
And comes out to friendly persons.

This cat sees a man with a van,
And she steps into the light,
"This cat is in too much pain," he says,
As she begs for a home with her eyes.

She was a sad soul,
With ticks that bit at her skin
The love that she had hidden in her heart,
Never showed until now.

She became ours,
An old girl she was
With no tail
No home and no one to turn to.

And because she was the cat
Who was found in The Ivy,
She was given the name of 'Ivy'
And then she became happy,
She knew that she was now home.

Alleena Purchase (13)
Steiner Academy Exeter, Exeter

My View On Poems: A Rap Battle

*S.O.P is the Society of Poetry

"I think poems are boring!
They are just things that are gnawing
Into my brain, the endless rhythmless ring,
The way they move around,
The way they feel and sound.
They're just a bunch of words lost or found."

"Well, I think quite differently in fact,
They pierce into you like *boom shaka-lack*"
But your courage, strength and power
I think you lack!
Because all you do is play on your Mac."

"The only thing they're good for is to fill you with dismay"

"English please, anglais, anglais!
What you just said was rude, okay?
It's a word which is hated by democracy-
You'll get arrested by the S.O.P*!"

"Let me interrupt you for a sec,
If what you said was true,
I'll get rickety wrecked!
Let us end this joke,
Before I start to choke
Upon this matter, I'd like you to evoke!"

"What did we learn from this argument?"

"I don't even know what the conversation really meant!"

"From this happening again, we shall prevent,
By shouting out that poetry does matter,
Ready on three guys, one, two, three..."

"Poetry can't be better!"

Teo 'YoungBlood' Hine (11)

Steiner Academy Exeter, Exeter

Animal Extinction

Sea turtles, loving, caring, swift and sweet,
Killed by rubbish dropped into the sea
There are also the otters,
Through the rivers, they swim,
Sleek, graceful and speedy,
Water pollution endangers their species.
Pandas are cuddly, soft and funny
Lack of food and places to live
Could make the pandas extinct.
Rhinos are gentle, caring and strong,
But poached for their horns,
They may soon be gone.
There is also the condor,
A strong bird of prey,
The loss of habitat,
Could mark their last days.
The bees are hardworking, caring, lifesaving,
Without them, nature would not be amazing.
Snow leopards are without a doubt
The most beautiful creature inside and out.
Beautiful, majestic,
Hunted for beauty,
Surely they can't be facing extinction.
And there are the polar bears, kings of the ice,
Strong and powerful but also quite nice.

Starvation, ice melting,
Could this be their ending?
What would it be like without these creatures?
How can we try and save them?

Alitza Grace Daly (12)

Steiner Academy Exeter, Exeter

Dance Of Magic

Butterflies' wings thump to your heart
and your feet lift off the ground and into the air.

The dragon roars a strong cry that rumbles into silence
and the earth around you rises to the clouds,
where nothing can hold you back.

A phoenix rises from the ashes,
and screeches until its flames become a shining star,
And your wings set alight like the phoenix.

The gift of magic is a beautiful dance,
made by your will it is your power for the world to see
and cannot be taken.
Let it shine like your smile.

Kama Ballantyne (13)
Steiner Academy Exeter, Exeter

Sinister Beauty

A heartfelt gleam,
two golden hands,
three strands of delicacy,
rabbits in the burrows,
the storm in the gallows.

A victim in the flesh,
strained corset laces
to hide the abscess,
vanity a stone-cold killer,
self-esteem a casualty
in anguish and affliction.

A heart first flush in your hands,
warm, beating, frantic, winged,
music and blood,
a host, of golden daffodils;
beside the lake, beneath the trees,
fluttering and dancing
in the breeze.

Karina Gilbert (15)
Steiner Academy Exeter, Exeter

Spring

I see the creatures wake with joy
From the slumber they'd employed
They shout with glee and run about
While all the otters search for trout
And as the trees grow their leaves
The flowers unfurl awaiting the bees
As spring arrives, groups of deer
And flocks of birds reappear
As all the animals dance and sing
I shout with joy, "Oh, happy spring!"

Laisey Jackson (11)
Steiner Academy Exeter, Exeter

Trapped

Cornered. No visible exit,
Trapped, caged, imprisoned.
I'm stuck, lost and lonely,
What do I do?

Brain says run,
Heart says stay.
But being around you is torture.
What do I do?

It needs to stop,
I'm not sure how.
Please help me,
What do I do?

A glimmer of hope,
Shining like the sun,
Bursting through the clouds,
It's blinding me with its brightness.
I think I know what I need to do.

I grab it with both hands,
Head spinning, heart pounding,
My lungs are taking short stabs of air,
Knees knocking, hands shaking,
I know what I need to do.

Bethany Hammond (14)
The Wey Valley School, Weymouth

My Pretty, Little Dress

This dress, my dress,
So pretty and white; soon became a mess,
So much I really do stress.

I may seem shy,
But I won't run and cry,
I'll be happy, just for you!
I hope you don't notice it too...
This dress I wear,
Always brings the coldest stare.

This is all a mess,
Looking down upon my dress,
Made from guilt and shame,
No one to blame.

I don't dream,
Nightmares make me scream,
Maybe this is why,
I always scream and cry,
This dress I wear,
Always brings the coldest stare.

At night I lay awake,
Feel every jolt, every shake,
I don't want to cry,

But my joy has gone bye-bye!
This dress I wear,
Always brings the coldest stare.

Blood is flowing,
Cuts are showing,
The dress is growing,
Life is going.

At night this dress will go and shine,
While all I do is cry and whine,
This pain, it'll never go away,
It's here to stay...

Oliwia Schodowski (14)
The Wey Valley School, Weymouth

Rainbow-Hearted

It's a strange feeling,
Not knowing who I am.

The lies are pretty,
The truth is ugly;
Washing away my rainbow heart,
One hue at a time.

I felt a brush against my hand,
And suddenly everything seemed clear.
The colours suppressed for a lifetime,
Bursting at the gentle touch.

The touch from her was so brief, so bare,
And I longed for more,
But I couldn't help but wonder:
"Is this okay?"

Am I allowed to feel this way?

Georgia-Louise Dorothy Genge (15)
The Wey Valley School, Weymouth

I Am Nothing

I listen, I am there
But does anyone notice me
I am the nerve in your brain that says
'Is that necessary?
Is that what you want people to do to you?'
But no one listens, no one ever listens
Except maybe a few if lucky.

I have to sit there and watch people dying
People's houses and families being bombed
Even people being racist about the people around us
But I can't, I can't escape.

No one says sorry, no one puts it right
But in the world, there is a little group of people
That are just like me, trying to help
But they just get ignored
But they are not like me, they are human
Like everyone else

If the world listens to me and the group of people
We won't have to escape or flee our homes
We don't have to try and escape reality
We can be who we are and stop escaping

Stop it, we are all human
Are you really who you are?

Evie Lou Daniel (14)
Trinity School, Teignmouth

Colours

She wanders
Her shoes torn and tattered
Her arms and hands scarred
Her face holds no expression
Her only belongings, she wears on her back
The responsibility to take care of her younger
Brothers at the front of her mind.

She opens her eyes
It was just a dream,
No, more of a memory
A monumental event which moulded her life
She climbs out of bed,
The distant colours of the cramped dinghy
Cloud her mind.

The colours are loud,
They are shouting at her
Screaming
The colours are less vibrant, but still there.

A constant reminder of what she was,
Of what they were.
Her label has changed.
No long a fourteen-year-old school girl,
A good Muslim girl, kind and caring.

Helpful
Now she was given a new label.

One splattered with the less vibrant colours
Of the cramped dinghy.
Her new label was just one word
One word would cause this
This word gave her no respect, dignity
Or equality.
One word gave people the right to shout
Abuse at her in the street.

For once the prejudice was not
For her skin tone but for her headscarf.
The religion she had followed from birth.
Everyone looked past the good she had done.
A grade A student, whose family gave to the poor.

They only saw the scar
They could only hear the media narrative
With no evidence of who she really was
They gave her a new label.

This word brought the colours back
But not the colours of her old life
But the colours of the bombing
Which killed her parents,

The colours of the trafficking from country
To country,
Colours of the abuse both mental and physical.

This word gave her colours,
Colours she had to bare.
Not bright, happy colours
Helpful, kind and caring,
All the values she had.

The ability for you to label something
Gives you clarity
But receiving the label makes you
Isolated, worthless, scared,
Depressed, stupid, inadequate,
Anxious, poor and different.

Different scares you.
These were the colours of her label,
Her new label
This one word
Terrorist.

Lottie Brown (14)
Trinity School, Teignmouth

Look Closer

And if you peered closer,
If you looked deep into her eyes,
You would notice the hurt, the pain she carries,
Her brown eyes could swallow you up whole,
They could transport you into her world,
Her world of mass destruction,
They could show you father turning on mother,
Government turning on the innocent,
Her society looking but not caring,
Watching but not taking action.

She lives in a world, a world that does not take recognition,
Recognition for the devastation it causes,
She witnesses death through addiction,
Abuse through the bottle and lives ruined with a syringe,
And all she can do is stare,
Stare in horror at the world she lives in.

She questions the sanity,
She watches in desperation,
She yearns to help,
But she is only one voice,
One voice embedded in a sea of corruption and ignorance.

Nevroz Turkmen (14)
Trinity School, Teignmouth

Escape

Lice crawl all over our bodies,
Even under the socks.
Men shiver violently.
Trench foot has swarmed us.
The trenches are simply mud
Dug for our graves.
I need to escape.

Rat-tat-tat!
The machine guns rattle rigorously,
Whoosh, bang!
Artillery strikes like lightning.
All of a sudden, I hear a siren.
Men are going over the top.
I need to escape.

Click.
I hear Lee-Enfield rifles reloading quickly.
Click-boom!
Grenades fly, killing men fast.
Men are being gunned down.
The machine guns shred us to pieces.
I need to escape.

Argh!
I hear men screaming, even this war is too hard for them.
Whoosh!

Planes swoop the war-torn skies.
Suddenly, I see birds.
This isn't their war to be fighting.
I need to escape.

Keep pushing men!
I hear officers yell. I see an escape route!
Past the trenches,
Into the nearest town of safety.
Once I'm there, I am safe!
I hope I can escape!

Rat-tat-tat!
Suddenly, I am gunned down by a machine gun.
The colour is draining from my face.
I am losing consciousness.
I am just another name and number to them.
I can no longer escape.

I am looking at my grandfather's grave,
A hundred years on,
11th November 2018,
It reads;
Henry N.J Gunther
11th November 1918
He was the last death in the war.
Remember all those who died
Because they can't escape.

Bertie Sweet (14)
Trinity School, Teignmouth

Why?

Born into this despicable world
Another husk for the guillotine that is society.
A world so bitter, that people can only find relief
In syringes and bottles.
Where you would rather know technology than people.
A place where wars are fought just because they are
'Other'
'Different'
'Unique'
I look out onto this world and feel disappointed
Disappointed by how a footballer can earn fortunes,
More than those creating our future and curing our
diseases.
I look out onto this world and feel sad
Sad for those who would rather ask for help
From a god in the sky than another person.
I look out onto this world and wonder
Wonder why the mind is so naturally greedy.
How a person can feast and another starve.
How one can have an empire and another the smallest
shack.
From the moment we exist,
We are forced into money-driven, pitiful lives
Where self-reliance is no longer an option,
And we seek only the next pay cheque and not a reason to
exist.

When humanity relies on goals and achievements
To give us meaning why not achieve peace?

Toby Roberts (14)
Trinity School, Teignmouth

Racism

Racism, it's everywhere,
There is nothing you can do,
Or can you?
It all starts with you,
Just that one individual
Who doesn't discriminate where people came from
Doesn't discriminate for the colour of your skin
But simply sees the beauty within,
The complex works of a human being
No different to you or me.

Strip back the bodies, just leave the souls on Earth
Nobody would discriminate
Or hate,
Or judge,
About the souls that are left behind
When they are not bound to a body they did not choose,
Features they cannot change from birth,
Destined to be abused, to lose,
When there is nothing they can do,
For things we cannot change
Are what we are judged on,
And it's a message to you,
Stop judging people for things they cannot choose
Or do anything about.

Treat them with respect,
And let your love flow out.

Henry Gates (14)
Trinity School, Teignmouth

Equality

Imagine feeling as if there is nowhere left to turn
You are stuck in this world of torment and fear
Feeling like you're not living, just breathing
As if you have been chained up, imprisoned in your own body
Feeling worthless and ashamed
Needing nothing more than to escape and be free
Society is cruel, people live in fear
Of people that are simply different.
People who are just a different race, gender, religion or sexuality.
People even try to hide behind the screens
Bully, intimidate, discriminate people
For trying to express who they are
If only the world could grow to accept us
For who we are, not what they see.

Eva Hunt (13)
Trinity School, Teignmouth

Down And Up

Nothing built can last forever,
Everything and everyone seems upside down
But does that stop us?
No, no matter how big the barricade seems
No matter which race, religion, weight or disability
We won't give in!
For the darkness and gloom that surrounds some
Isn't as big as you think.
The light to break through to freedom isn't far at all.
Just one step.
You can make it - you have just got to believe!
Anything is possible if you believe.
Even the impossible.
Everything might be complicated right now,
But we are down and up, rather than up and down.

Tom Nicol (13)
Trinity School, Teignmouth

The Mind

Slowly, I close my eyes
Dreading the thought of being alone
Being alone.

My mind is in a war
The arrows my mistakes
The bombs my inner fears, holding back tears
I still have the feeling of being alone.
Being alone.

I feel as if I'm at a fairground
My emotions on a roller coaster,
Happy, sad, afraid
As I scroll through my memories
Still being alone.

I can't wait to wake
For goodness sake
I don't want to sleep
Because I keep feeling
The overwhelming fear
Of being alone.

Lily Marder (15)
Trinity School, Teignmouth

No Escape

If you want to escape society, you can't!
The world is a cruel, abusive place
It does not matter how hard you try
Society will just spit you back out
If you try and make the world better
It will not work, nothing will change!
Life is life!
If what happens to you,
Is bad or good, you will just have to deal with it
Step, by step.
Once you complete one step, move onto the next
And do this until you are too tired to do anymore.
Remember to craft your future!

Oliver Protheroe (13)
Trinity School, Teignmouth

Oasis

A haiku

Oasis, freedom.
Glowing shards of moonlit dreams,
Resting in God's palm.

Tom Timoney-White (15)
Trinity School, Teignmouth

YoungWriters®
Est. 1991

YOUNG WRITERS
INFORMATION

We hope you have enjoyed reading this book – and
that you will continue to in the coming years.

If you're a young writer who enjoys reading and creative
writing, or the parent of an enthusiastic poet or story writer,
do visit our website **www.youngwriters.co.uk**. Here you
will find free competitions, workshops and games, as well
as recommended reads, a poetry glossary and our blog.
There's lots to keep budding writers motivated to write!

If you would like to order further copies of this book,
or any of our other titles, then please give us
a call or visit **www.youngwriters.co.uk**.

Young Writers
Remus House
Coltsfoot Drive
Peterborough
PE2 9BF
(01733) 890066
info@youngwriters.co.uk

Join in the conversation!
Tips, news, giveaways and much more!

 YoungWritersUK    @YoungWritersCW